PRAISE FOR HADRIANA IN ALL MY DREAMS

"The sights and sounds of Haiti's vibrant carnival season invigorate this tale of vodou and Haitian culture... The truth of Hadriana's fate proves more poignant than horrifying, but in Depestre's hands, this incident is a touchstone of a culture in which distinctions between the empirical and spiritual are obscured, and whose traditional celebrations and beliefs introduce an element of the mythic into the everyday. Eroticism and humour course through his narrative. Depestre's intimacy with his subject matter and his familiarity with the people he portrays—the story is set in his hometown, at the time when he was 12 years old—give readers an insider's look at Jacmelian culture."

—*Publisher's Weekly*

"One-of-a-kind... [A] ribald, free-wheeling magical-realist novel, first published in 1988 and newly, engagingly translated by Glover... An icon of Haitian literature serves up a hotblooded, rib-ticking, warmhearted mélange of ghost story, cultural inquiry, folk art, and *véritable l'amour*."

—*Kirkus Reviews* (starred review)

"It would take a long time to unwrap the many layers of 1   rangely
hau   was born
in t   he so

vividly describes here... By contrasting Haitian vodou with traditional Christianity, and pitting colour and class lines against each other, Depestre presents a rich and nuanced exploration of large and significant themes expertly couched in one fantastical, expertly translated tale."

—*Booklist* (starred review)

"For the first time, this slim and beguiling novel about the mysterious death and possible zombification of a young woman on her wedding day has been translated into English... With its lyrical commentary on the origins of myth, this mesmeric and frequently erotic work transcends its focus on a young woman to address the complexities of race, class and religion."

—*Shelf Awareness for Readers*, (starred review)

"Originally published in 1988 and written by one of Haiti's seminal authors, still with us at age 90, this vibrant, erotically charged work shows how humans counter fear—particularly the fear of death—in varied more or less magical ways, even as it paints a fresh and enticing picture of Haitian culture... Luscious and affirmative reading, this is work both the serious-minded and the lighthearted can enjoy."

—*Library Journal* (starred review)

"*Hadriana In All My Dreams* is a compelling monograph. Surreal and imaginative, it is written with a dark richness and poignancy that is void of sensationalism and hyperbole. This is fictional realism at its best, and author Rene Depestre proves his salt as a master craftsman."

"Depestre, a grandfather of Haitian literature, spins a sensuous romp that serves up equal helpings of the historically contemplative and the handsomely entertaining... *Hadriana in All My Dreams* opens its narrative palm cheekily, cleverly, to reveal the kernel-truth of Jacmelian life, of a resurrected beauty's power beyond pulchritude. It's a story that contains its own universe, tucked irresistibly into an evening's riotous, ruddy-cheeked read... suitable for sneaking into weddings and funerals alike."

"Zombies, voodoo, and a sex-crazed boy–turned-butterfly are all facts of everyday life in Depestre's... colourful, magic-suffused novel."

"The story is an extended love letter to author René Depestre's hometown, its creole culture, its architecture, and its annual Carnival. Visitors to Jacmel can trace the exact route of the narrative through the streets of the town, and next to the crumbling, stately mansion Depestre depicted as Hadiana's manor, a public staircase is decorated with a mosaic spelling out the opening lines of the novel."

"A slim and beautiful novel about death, sex, and

Haitian myth... A dreamlike novel that blends eye-witness testimony to the possible zombification of Hadriana with the villagers' erotic and fanciful half-memories of Haiti's thorny history."

—Kaiama L. Glover (translator), *Chicago Review*

"The story is beautifully written in lyrical prose... Readers interested in Haitian culture will appreciate this novel and will enjoy Depestre's details about the voodoo culture as it was understood in the first half of the 20th century."

—*Historical Novels Review*

"An exceptional novel... Depestre's masterpiece and one of the greatest examples of Haitian literature."

—*New York Journal of Books*

"The most important thing a work-in-translation can offer a reader [is] perspective on a place, people, and language we don't immediately have access to, or one that runs counter to conventional, cliché narratives. Glover's book does that in aces."

—*Words Without Borders*

"You've never read about a zombie like Hadriana. Transformed into the walking dead on her wedding day, Hadriana becomes part of popular legend, one imbued with magic, eroticism, and even humour."

—Tor.com

"You do not need to believe in zombies or Vodou to be carried away by this story—a metaphor for all forms of dispossession... René Depestre has gone beyond nostalgia to write a sumptuous love story."

—*Le Monde*

HADRIANA

IN ALL

MY DREAMS

René Depestre

Translated by Kaiama L. Glover

with introduction by
Edwidge Danticat

JACARANDA

This edition first published in Great Britain 2020 by
Jacaranda Books Art Music Ltd
27 Old Gloucester Street
London, UK WC1N 3AX
www.jacarandabooksartmusic.co.uk

This translation originally published in English in the United States
by Akashic Books, New York 2017

Originally published in French under the title *Hadriana Dans Tous
Mes Reves* by Editions Gallimard, Paris, France 1988

A CIP catalogue record for this book is available from the British
Library

ISBN: 9781909762732
eISBN: 9781909762749

Typeset by Kamillah Brandes
Cover design by Rodney Dive

INTRODUCTION

BY EDWIDGE DANTICAT

WHAT IS IT that sends us on a quest to describe what René Depestre calls "*surréalisme quotidien*" or the daily mysteries of life? The misconstrued nature of a subject is certainly a powerful draw. One must be daring, though, to speak for the dead. The real conversation between spirit and flesh most likely takes place in some undefined realm, a place neither here nor there, where the soul pounds into the body—or flees the body—in a way that only some among the living can fully understand.

René Depestre seems to be one of those who understands. In *Hadriana in All My Dreams*, he makes himself a bridge between the living and the dead and offers us the kind of tale we rarely get in the hundreds of zombie stories featuring Haitians. In *Hadriana in All My Dreams* we get *langaj*—the secret language of Haitian Vodou—as well as the type of descriptive, elegiac, erotic, and satirical language, and the artistic license needed, to create this most nuanced and powerful novel. And on top of all that, we also witness one of Haiti's most popular carnivals in the beautiful southern coastal town of Jacmel, where our story takes place.

To offer a plot summary here would be to remove from the reader the great pleasure of discovering with fresh eyes this most stimulating and unpredictable novel. I can only assure you that you are in good hands with Depestre. Just as one might at carnival, one must surrender to this story while not being too easily offended or outraged.

René Depestre was born in Jacmel in 1926 and is one of Haiti's best-known writers. Even though he has been living outside of the country for over half a century, he drew upon his childhood memories of the 1938 carnival season for this novel, first published in French in 1988. Depestre began his writing career as a poet at the young age of nineteen, and his poetic tendencies are on full display here. His fluid use of at times lyrical, at times whimsical, and at times academic language, as well as his inclusion of vivid erotica, shows him also to be a hybrid writer, unafraid to take risks either with word usage or subject matter. The novel occasionally veers into lodyans—a tongue-in-cheek narrative genre meant to provoke laughter, though here perhaps it is intended to provoke other carnal reactions as well.

When I first read this novel, I was researching a non fiction book about carnival in Jacmel. I had visited the town many times and was captivated by its colourful history and distinct architecture, some of which is meticulously portrayed here. *Hadriana* soon became the centrepiece of my book. Quotations from the novel became the epigraph to nearly every chapter. I loved the way this novel bound hyperrealism and magical realism—or, as Alejo Carpentier, one of Depestre's inspirations, called it, the real *maravilloso*, or the marvellous real. Also magical and marvellous is how much the southern town of Jacmel itself takes centre stage in *Hadriana*. Depestre is Jacmelian and proud of it; he not only describes a lively town, but also evokes class, colour, religion, and gender dynamics, cleverly weaving them into his supernatural plot. He name-drops famous Jacmelians whom locals, and even regular visitors, are likely to recognize.

The quotidian surrealism is depicted in such precise and

exacting detail that human butterflies and zombies on the loose barely startle some folks. Still, Depestre is not one of those writers the narrator critiques. I'm referring to those who fail to realize that we might never fully grasp the intangible, even when we come face to face with some physical manifestation thereof: a person who is not really a person, a spirit who is not really a spirit, but who exists in a gap that few are able to portray without slipping into lazy stereotypes and easy generalizations about Haitian life and the country's religions and complex, nuanced culture.

The fact that we continue to be bombarded with the same old pedestrian zombie narratives written by foreigners and featuring Haitians makes this novel even more crucial, and this beautiful and masterful translation by Kaiama L. Glover extremely welcome. Here is how it might be done, Depestre seems to be telling us, within a singular and exceptional community. Still, Depestre does not shy away from showing the ways that a town, or a country, as he has stated in several interviews, can become zombified through repression, desperation, fear, and neglect.

"Is it possible that my homeland was some sort of collective zombie?" the narrator asks himself. "Behind each mystery," he concludes, "there were at least a hundred more."

You will find at least a hundred more mysteries beyond the obvious story told in *Hadriana in All My Dreams*. This novel is also a story of migration—the type of migration that many Haitians are forced to make, either by land, air, or sea, when all doors at home are closed to them. Perhaps the part of us that would like to remain with our families, in our own countries, perhaps that part of us must die in order for us to be "reborn" elsewhere. This novel is in many ways reminiscent of Jean Rhys's *Wide Sargasso Sea*, except in this case Depestre's white Creole woman refuses to become a prisoner, and the precursor to Depestre's novel is not another novel, but the wider zombie canon, a genre Depestre subtly tries to both deconstruct and rewrite with this book.

Our narrator writes:

> In each text I read on Vodou, there was the obligatory chapter on zombies in Haiti. In every instance, the author seemed somehow to be left short of breath, chasing after an elusive ghost. There was a time when the flood of studies on this element of Haitian sorcery constituted a veritable industry, both within and outside the academic world. It went from the most frenzied sensationalism to the most erudite scholarship. I wanted to offer a personal perspective, situated somewhere between a serialized novel and a monograph—some new and well-thought-out, passionate, and organized tribute to my beloved—that I hoped would raise the debate to a higher plane.

As you will soon discover in the pages of this magnificent novel, both the writer René Depestre and *Hadriana*'s narrator have more than succeeded.

ABOUT THE AUTHOR

Edwidge Danticat is the award-winning author of *Breath, Eyes, Memory* (an Oprah's Book Club selection), *Krik? Krak!*, *The Dew Breaker*, *Brother, I'm Dying*, and several other books. She is the editor of four anthologies, including *Haiti Noir* and *Haiti Noir 2: The Classics*.

Hadriana
in all my
Dreams

René Depestre

Translated by Kaiama L. Glover

For Nelly, Paul-Alain, and Stefan.
In memory of André Breton and Pierre Mabille.

We have only one recourse in the face of death: make art before it happens.
—René Char

FIRST MOVEMENT

CHAPTER ONE

BALTHAZAR AND THE SEVEN LOINS OF MADAME VILLARET-JOYEUSE

Lord, heap miseries upon us
yet entwine our arts with laughters low.
—James Joyce

1

THAT YEAR, TOWARD the end of my childhood, I was living in Jacmel, a coastal village in Haiti. When my father died, my mother and I moved from La Gosseline Avenue to go live with my maternal uncle. Thanks to his position as magistrate, he and his wife resided in a bright and spacious dwelling on Bourbon Street, in Bel-Air. On public holidays, during the most blistering hours of the day, I used to take my sorrows out for a little air on the balcony of their wood-frame house. I'd wait for something to catch my eye, to distract me enough for my imagination to wander off into daydreams.

One Sunday in October, in the middle of the afternoon, a car suddenly caught my attention—it was driving slowly down our street, and from my spot on the balcony, I could make out two people inside.

"What do you see there?" asked Mam Diani.

"A convertible."

"Whose car is it?"

"I've never seen it before."

"Really?... And the passengers?"

"A lady and her driver."

"A lady out and about in this heat?"

The car came closer, its motor humming gently. On both sides of the road, our neighbours were already out on their verandas or peering out of their windows. Like my mother and me, they too were curious about this new development.

"A cabriolet, a sedan, a coupé?" asked my mother.

"A limousine, pearl-gray, brand new!"

"And the lady, for heaven's sake, who is she?"

"It's my godmother, Madame Villaret-Joyeuse. Lil' Jérôme is at the wheel."

"Hush your mouth, Patrick! Germaine Muzac is on her death bed!"

My dream car was right there before my eyes. Lil' Jérôme Villaret-Joyeuse was wearing a beige silk shirt, a pair of navy-blue pants, and a Panama hat. His normally cheerful and boyish Caribbean face had taken on the tragic mask of someone executing a daunting task. His mother was seated in the middle of the backseat, with a large Chinese fan in one hand and a chambray handkerchief in the other. She had on a mauve dress with a lace collar, closed with a silver brooch. The sleeves came to her elbows and had organdy flounces. At her neck, a gold chain held an ivory crucifix, and her earrings and bracelets sparkled. She was bareheaded but carefully coiffed. She had the lips, nose, and cheeks of a perfectly healthy person. But her eyebrows, which she had always kept arched and very full, had grown excessively—right up to the very top of her forehead and all around her eyes. They formed a giant moth; the antennae, body, and delicate silver scales of butterfly wings were clearly visible. It looked sort of like a carnival mask, covering half her face and made of velvet, or satin. To what masked ball could my godmother possibly be headed in this relentless mid afternoon heat?

"Mercy! Have mercy on us!" said my mother, who made the sign of the cross before looking up at me in consternation. "Patrick, get down there and follow them."

I obeyed without hesitation. The car turned onto Church

Street toward the northern side of the town's central square, Place d'Armes (also known as Toussaint Louverture Square). All of a sudden, everyone on the surrounding balconies was paralyzed with shock. General Télébec, the hundred-year-old parrot that lived in the prefecture, constantly on alert for the latest gossip, fell right off his perch and then took off, screaming: "Help, help—it's the end of the world!"

The neighbourhood dogs joined the chorus. Brutally awakened from his nap, Jacmel's prefect, Barnabé Kraft, rushed to the steps of the building, still in his silk pyjamas.

"Forgive me, my dear Germaine!" the prefect shouted at the car. "*Bravissimo!* You're in fine shape, aren't you? Hush, Télébec, you won't fare well at the court martial!"

At the Star Café, run by Didi Brifas, the regulars who played cards on the terrace just sat there facing their fellow card players, arms dangling and mouths agape.

"Damnation, Lil' Jérôme!" were the only words Togo Lafalaise managed to utter.

Lil' Jérôme appeared indifferent to the general panic. It seemed like nothing in the world was more important to him than the curved path he was taking between the square and the Saint Rose of Lima School for nuns. The sisters greeted his car with signs of the cross. Several of them threw themselves to their knees in the establishment's sunny inner courtyard. One of them cut a flower and threw it over the fence.

Past the trees of Lovers Lane, the car continued on to the Siloé family manor. Built down below the square, the house's third floor windows were even with the height of the overhanging esplanade, which the car had just begun to pass. So it was Hadriana Siloé, opening the Venetian blinds of her bedroom windows, who found herself with a prime seat from which to watch the passing of the woman who, at an interval of three years, had held both of us over the same baptismal font. My godsister rubbed her eyes before crying out: "Godmother, wait, my love, I'm coming down!"

Upon hearing the young French girl, instead of braking, Lil' Jérôme accelerated his descent toward Orléans Street, which ran alongside the Siloés' garden. I took off in a cloud of dust and finally caught up with the car right in front of the prison, where Lil' Jérôme had slowed down to a funereal pace. At the entrance to the penitentiary, the guard, stunned, presented his Springfield rifle with great ceremony, as if the lovely Villaret-Joyeuse were some high-ranking police official.

At the very bottom of the steep coast, after a corkscrew turn, the warehouses on the docks came into sight. We passed in front of the ochre-coloured buildings of the customs house and the tax offices. We reached a paved platform where on weekdays hundreds of women sang as they sorted the coffee for the Radsen brothers' export business. Once there, Lil' Jérôme slowed down even more, as if to allow the living butterfly mask that had taken the place of his mother's eyes a chance to enjoy the fabulous brilliance of the sun glistening on the coconut trees, the wild grasses and boulders of the coast, and the roiling waves of the bay. The weather was heavenly. In different circumstances, the romantic adolescent that I was back then would have saluted the beauty of the world with unbridled cries, while dancing and rolling on the ground in jubilation. Instead, tears came to my eyes and my knees buckled beneath me as the limousine dragged me along, helpless as I was in the face of death.

Taking Seafront and Réunion streets, Lil' Jérôme quickly arrived in the Bas des Orangers neighbourhood, located in one of the remote areas of Jacmel. We moved forward among the dilapidated cottages that were piled up helter-skelter along the alleys overrun by weeds and potholes. A few shirtless men played dominoes, while hordes of children followed a paper canoe race in the sewer water. Seated on very low chairs, thighs parted, a few matronly women furiously deloused some howling little girls. Three young women, their six breasts exposed, competed to see who could produce the strongest stream of milk. An old man, using a shard from a broken bottle, shaved a young boy's head, the glass scraping closely along the scalp. Stacked chaotically in the shade of the verandas, families, dogs, cats, and chickens all killed time Haitian-style on this October Sunday.

Suddenly, a terrified voice rose above the din of Estaing Alley: "Zombie car on the loose!"

It was every man for himself in the courtyard. Panicked, all God's children somehow lost all sense of time: it could just as easily have been three thirty in the afternoon or three thirty in the morning, 1938 or 38 BC. Five hundred meters farther, completely out of breath, I felt like I had succeeded in making my way back to the month of October—and to the twentieth century—upon reaching the main street that turned onto La Gosseline Avenue where the Villaret-Joyeuse family resided. Lil' Jérôme sped through the gate, and I found myself terribly alone in the disquiet of a deserted neighbourhood, where the extraordinary had just erupted into all of our lives.

2

Jacmel gave Germaine Villaret-Joyeuse a funeral worthy of her renown. In the weeks that followed, the strange events of that October weekend gave way to frenetic collective myth-making. One early evening, a bunch of us young people crowded around a bench on Toussaint Louverture Square to listen to the hairdresser Scylla Syllabaire's detailed account of the events—which ended up being accepted as the official truth.

On the morning of her death, Germaine had gathered together those closest to her to hear her final wishes. She had just had a strikingly prophetic dream in which it had been revealed to her that, up in heaven, purgatory and paradise were separated by a bay exactly like the one in Jacmel. So, she desired only one thing to happen at the moment of her passing: to get a precise sense of the distance that her soul would have to travel in order to access eternal bliss at the end of her earthly trials.

"My darling son," she said to Lil' Jérôme, "drive me to the port. If I should die before we arrive, make sure to place that butterfly mask over my eyes. You know the one I mean. Yes, my dear, the butterfly will be leaving with me. Let him look at the bay in my place. It is fitting that a queen should appear masked before our merciful Christ."

Reassured by her own words, Germaine Muzac passed

away at that very moment. What was to be done with such a final wish? This was the subject of a brief debate among her family members.

"Mama was very weak," said Erica. "In her state, she could just as easily have dreamed of a trip in a hot-air balloon or a hydroplane to lead her to the waters of Saint Pierre. We don't have to pay her any mind."

Lil' Jérôme didn't agree. Their mother had entrusted him with a sacred mission. He would execute it if it meant burning down the whole house, the town of Jacmel, or the entire island. Before the terrified eyes of his family members, he invited that diabolical winged half-breed, with its skull and crossbones for a head, to come down from its spot on the ceiling and settle upon the eyes of the dead woman. Then, once she had been washed, exfoliated, made up, clothed in her ceremonial dress, and adorned with her jewels, his mother was placed in the backseat of the car and propped up with some cushions.

Scylla Syllabaire went on to recount the story of that escapade. From the very beginning, his story did not match up with what I had so excitedly seen with my own two eyes and ears along the course of that promenade. According to Scylla, Télébec, the state's propagandistic parrot, had stood up to the butterfly and exclaimed bravely: "There it is, the unholy beast! Ready, aim, fire!"

In reality, General Télébec had fallen from his perch and then fled as fast as his wings would carry him, all the while crying out: "Help, help—it's the end of the world!" Forty years later I can still hear the racket he and the dogs made.

Scylla similarly distorted the prefect's words and the actions of the nuns. And it was not true, according to Scylla, that an old woman from Bas des Orangers had screamed: "Zombie car on the loose!" Instead, Scylla claimed to have heard from a local resident on Raquette Street that a little blind girl had been the first person from the slums to sound the alarm, crying out: "Beware the messenger of death!"

His evocation of Hadriana Siloe's appearance on the scene was even further from the truth than what I had seen with my own eyes. According to the hair-dresser, Lil' Jérôme had stopped short when he saw André Siloé's heaven-sent daughter appear at the manor's window. An instant later, she was at the car, placing a goodbye kiss on her godmother's forehead. Hadriana was naked from head to toe, marvellously and entirely naked—her virgin flesh, just below the navel, was an absolute wonder! The butterfly was completely dazzled by it, his antennae paralyzed. In all his wanderings around the islands, never before had he seen such a superbly inviting conch between any young girl's thighs. If you put it up to your ear, you would hear the Caribbean Sea! And so it was that he lost all desire to escort Germaine Muzac to paradise. What would be the point of dying? What the hell was he doing on the sightless eyes of the godmother when there remained such a vibrant light to bask in within the goddaughter's womb? Wings a-quiver, he launched himself on the path to glory.

In the very same breath, Scylla Syllbaire revealed to us that the butterfly that all of Jacmel had seen laid across the eyes of the dead woman was in fact a human being like you and me. His name was Balthazar Granchiré. Born some twenty years earlier in the mountains of Cap-Rouge, his mother and father unknown, he had been found in the middle of the street just a few hours after his birth. The infamous sorcerer Okil Okilon had adopted the infant. On the day of his twelfth birthday, he had been precociously initiated into the *Vlanbindingues*, a secret society in southwestern Haiti. From that moment on, a passion for sex turned the adolescent into the most sex-crazed womaniser in the country. At the age of fifteen, he already counted about a hundred women, of all ages, among his conquests. A year later, he seduced his adoptive father's *femme-jardin*. Okilon took revenge for this affront: he turned his rival into a butterfly, all the while showering curses on him.

"You ungrateful, motherless little boy. I condemn you to the category of the most loathsome half-breeds of the Caribbean. Your upper wings will be reddish-brown with blue spots and black streaks. Your posterior wings will have all shades of ochre, their honey-coloured outer edges adorned with a thin strip of mauve. Your abdomen will be cylindrical, striped with black and lemon yellow. You'll have blue-green circles around your eyes and your irises will be perfectly suited for a devil of your kind. Your nine-inch wingspan will be exceptional, even among *bizango* butterflies. And when you fly, you'll leave behind a shimmering trail, more twisted and zigzagging than a flash of lightning.

"On the dorsal part of your thorax, you'll have violet, eye-shaped circles, a malachite-green moustache, a canary-yellow mouth, a square chin, the overall air of some godless bandit of a white man—a goddamned skull and crossbones! Your phenomenal erect member will continue to grow every time it ejaculates into the cunts it assaults. Curled up into a serrated spiral, your cursed watch-spring will mark the instant of ecstasy on the flesh of its prey, leaving each victim desperate to savour that moment for all eternity. Old grandfather clocks that stopped working years earlier will start ticking again thanks to your machine gun of a dick, but the hands of your clock will move in opposite direction to a woman's true lunar cycle.

"You'll be more bloodthirsty in your vaginal dealings than a praying mantis. You'll devour them before, during, and after copulation. You'll take pleasure in quenching your thirst with the tears of virgins and widows. Your antennae will pick up the scent of menstrual blood from a mile away. You'll waste your sperm chasing after females. You'll swing uncontrollably from the gentleness of a hummingbird to the ferocity of a Bengal tiger. Unzipping your fly, women will find themselves facing a daunting crankshaft with a nightmare-seeking head for a knob. The most captivating orgasms will wreak havoc on the otherwise pleasant lives that your devil of a phallus will have bent to its mercy. Goddamned satyr—you and your zombifying *zozo*, get the hell out of Okil Okilon's garden!"

3

BALTHAZAR GRANCHIRÉ ARRIVED in Jacmel for the first
time in November 1936, only eight weeks after the passage
of Hurricane Bethsabée, in a town still trying to tend to its
wounds. He took up residence in one of the silk-cotton trees
on Toussaint Louverture Square. On the night of his arrival,
he deflowered the Philisbourg twins during their sleep and
Sister Nathalie-des-*Anges*, one of the nuns from the Saint
Rose of Lima School. This was the first time he tested the
strategy he would come to perfect over the course of the
next few months. He would wait until nightfall to slip into
a bedroom and then hide out under the bed. Once his prey
had fallen asleep, he would fill the air with his aphrodisiac
exhalations. A few minutes later, breasts would be popping
the buttons on nightgowns, bottoms bursting the elastic of
underwear, enflamed thighs opening wide, vaginas, fascinated,
crying out with thirst and, above all, hunger. At that point,
all Balthazar would have to do was launch his campaign.
Superb adolescents, having gone to bed virgins, safe within
the cocoon of the family, would awaken dismayed, with blood
everywhere, brutally deflowered. At first, the appalled family
members would attribute this rash of domestic despoiling to a
delayed effect of the devastating hurricane. (This explanation
fizzled out pretty quickly, though.)

On those mornings, the dreams that permeated the sleep

of the victims generally involved an episode of fabulous flight. Everyone remembered having flown in an airplane at a low altitude over the bay of Jacmel in an uninterrupted orgasm, in perfect weather. Each woman spoke of an aerial adventure that left her swooning with joy. But then, at the peak of excitement, the aircraft would transform into a gaping mouth, dramatically splitting open into an arc that snatched up everything in its path.

Lolita Philisbourg felt as if the folds of her own soft lips, open to the exact size of the skies above the bay, were violently enveloping the rest of her body. Her sister Klariklé felt her love tunnel open up beneath her like a trap door while her own father whispered in her ear that she should not have forgotten her parachute at home. Sister Nathalie-des-*Anges* saw her very Catholic cavern-of-the-Good-Lord impetuously competing with the frothy waves bubbling on the surface of the sea. Such was the calling card that Balthazar Granchiré left beneath the sheets.

Hoping to catch the incubus before his assaults, vigilant mothers sat at their daughters' bedsides, armed with steel mesh. The following morning they would discover to their dismay that they had succumbed, without even putting up a fight, to the same witchcraft as their innocent progeny. They, too, remembered flying just above the waves, whisked away by an orgasm that could only be described as miraculous.

Mrs. Eric Jeanjumeau confessed to Father Naélo that she had had six orgasms in one minute. Mrs. Émile Jonassa had come furiously thirteen times in a row. The widow Jastram's rapture had been a true classic of sensual pleasure: she promised herself to hold onto it beyond the dream so as to include it later in a sex-education manual. Unlike their little girls, instead of being thrown into a pit after the sex act, they had all seen their genitals laid out graciously on a ceremonial table in the midst of all sorts of sumptuously garnished platters. They had heard their own voices cry out: "Monsignor, dinner is served! Come get it while it's hot!"

Germaine Villaret-Joyeuse alone experienced an entirely different adventure on the wings of Granchiré. "And do you know why?" Syllabaire asked us, alternately blinking each of his eyes.

"Because of her loins!" we cried out in unison.

During my childhood, Germaine Villaret-Joyeuse's genital apparatus was an inevitable subject of off-colour jokes. We talked about it during wakes, banquets, wedding celebrations, baptisms, and First Communions. Popular gossip had it that my godmother possessed a veritable cascade of loins: two in her lower back, two in the front of her body, one to the left of her stomach, and two others, even more demanding, between her breasts. On the night of her first marriage, her spouse had been brought out on a stretcher, felled by a double fracturing of the pelvis. "Poor Anatole was in a condition not unlike someone who'd fallen from the very top of a coconut tree," confided Dr. Sorapal to my uncle Ferdinand, who was the magistrate called to investigate the damage.

The second husband, for his part, was admitted to St. Michel Hospital with several broken ribs. Only Archibald Villaret-Joyeuse, her third spouse, succeeded in avoiding these perils. The honeymoon left him safe and sound, ready to return to his flourishing fabric business. He managed to keep up marvellously with Germaine Muzac's legendary pelvic thrusts. He truly earned his nickname: Sir Archbishop-of-Joy. He gave his companion eight children in six years. And then he died in a manner completely unfamiliar to local doctors: a double bee sting to the testicles did him in within the space of twenty-four hours.

On the widow's forty-fifth birthday, in the *Southwest Gazette*, Maître Népomucène Homaire paid remarkable homage to his childhood friend:

> With her abundant charms and a genital apparatus like that at her disposal, she'll have no problem lasting to the year 2000. The reproductive power flowing through her body has the cool exuberance of a mountain waterfall. Germaine Muzac's fertile loins, twinkling with magical sparks, will make sure that male orgasms of the third millennium finish in a blaze of glory.

"With a power plant like that below the waist," commented my uncle Ferdinand, "in 2043 our dear Joyeuse will still be capable of taking our great-grandsons onto her aircraft for a trip to paradise!"

Meanwhile, according to Scylla Syllabaire, it was our old buddy General Granchiré who ended up saying how-do-you-do to the heavens! After each trip, Germaine woke up in perfect form, lit up from the inside by her thirty-six orgasms, and found herself facing her indefatigable butterfly. They swore never to leave one another. Their liaison brought several months of respite to the local families. There was no more talk of mysterious *deflowering*s, of cruelly interrupted engagements, of honeymoons shamelessly stolen from desperate young spouses, of wedding announcements cancelled last minute by Father Naélo.

Informed of the tragic fate that had left Granchiré lurching about like a drunkenly spinning top, Germaine planned to negotiate secretly with Okil Okilon for the return of her miraculous beast to his human condition. Offered a hefty payment, the sorcerer would consider having Balthazar undergo, in reverse, the metamorphosis that had served to exile him *ad vitam aeternam* to the kingdom of libertine lepidoptera. Once back in his chrysalis, Balthazar would return to the larval state and then follow the transformation of a caterpillar until finally reclaiming the physique and the freedom of the dashing young man he had once been.

That is where things stood when cancer in her right breast, having metastasised unbridled, tossed to the wind any other bells that had been tolling in my godmother's haunted loins. Eventually, the night came when she had only one loin left able to resist—like Leonidas I at the Battle of Thermopylae—both the onslaught of the malignant tumour and the "Persian Army" that was, for her alone, her lover's animal sensuality. Thoroughly moved by her immense heroism, Balthazar decided to render eternal the party he and Germaine had begun in Jacmel. One evening, he let her see in a dream the space between purgatory and Eden, a bay whose beauty resembled the area carved out by the Caribbean Sea in the Jacmelian coastline. He spread his seer's wings across the eyes of his immortal beloved, so that the wind would not lead them astray from their maritime path to heaven.

4

Scylla Syllabaire's tale left my friends and me breathless. He had quite a gift for misrepresenting the truth. What a bald-faced rearranging of reality! What was I waiting for—why was I not telling the truth that I had seen with my own eyes? Well, in those days, everyone in Jacmel knew better than to interrupt the gritty eloquence of Scylla Syllabaire's revelations. The hairdresser's mystically illuminated version won the day as far as Jacmel's imagination was concerned. I mean, were we not all perfectly willing to believe that Scylla was keeping three young Egyptian girls hidden away in his bachelor pad? Addressing us from the height of his own legendary sexual exploits, he bent our minds to the will of his fantasies. Nonetheless, I dared to pose, however cautiously, the question that burned on everyone's lips.

"If Granchiré had already 'popped' Nana Siloé," I said, "Father Naélo wouldn't have announced my godsister's marriage to Hector Danoze at midnight Mass on Christmas Eve. But he posted it right on the door of the church. The wedding is set for January 29."

"When it comes to white folks, people know how to keep a secret. Father Naélo and Danoze know nothing about any of this. Hector only knows that ever since losing Germaine's seven loins, the butterfly has been sniffing around his fiancée, unsuccessfully. And Hector has sworn to kill Balthazar before he ever gets a chance to cut any of Hadriana's sweet, sweet grass!"

"So Granchiré has no chance?"

"Look, he wasn't born yesterday. Just last Saturday, at dawn, he saw the happy couple walking down Lovers Lane. The young man was wearing a hunting rifle strapped across his chest—a Winchester semiautomatic, from what I've heard. He was whispering sweet nothings in his sweetheart's ear, but he had his eyes on the silk-cotton trees lining the square the whole time. Balthazar hightailed it out of there."

"And is that the last anyone's seen of him?"

"As of right now, he's retired to Cap-Rouge. He's staying in Rosalvo Rosanfer's sanctuary. Rosanfer is the head of the Brotherhood of the Zobops, and a rival of Okil Okilon; he's helping Balthazar make his wings resistant to Danoze's bullets. So he won't be gone for long. And when he returns, he'll be supernaturally endowed..."

CHAPTER TWO

THE STAR THAT SHINED BUT ONCE

I watched the death of the star that shined but once.
—Kateb Yacine

1

In the January 11, 1938 issue of the *Southwest Gazette*, the managing editor, Népomucène Homaire, devoted his entire editorial to the marriage of Hadriana Siloé and Hector Danoze:

We take the upcoming marriage of the young Frenchwoman Hadriana Siloé and our compatriot Hector Danoze to be a capital event. The families of the future spouses have obtained the consent of our city's fathers to turn these nuptials into a veritable public bacchanalia. After Hurricane Bethsabée, the crash of coffee prices on the world market, the terrorizing of local hymens by a savage woodland butterfly, and the recent death of Germaine Villaret-Joyeuse, the wedding of this mixed couple comes just in time to reunite Jacmel with the rhythms of life through dance and fantasy.

The religious ceremony at the Saint Philippe and Saint Jacques Church will be followed by a reception at the Siloé manor. That evening, the young bride and groom and their guests will join the entire population of Jacmel on Place d'Armes to take part in an unprecedented carnival celebration.

There are a few marriages that have remained famous in our county. Indeed, on more than one occasion we have witnessed two beings, filled with wonder for one another, decide to unite their beauty and their passion in a single destiny. But the wedding that will take place on Saturday, January 29, is sure to stand out in our annals for even more exceptional reasons.

Hadriana, the only daughter of the brilliant couple Denise and André Siloé, is the princely gift that the French nation of Debussy and Renoir has given to our country. Much more than a young girl of nineteen, the tutelary fairy of Jacmel is a rose plucked from the hat of the good Lord. In the absence of Isabelle Ramonet, residing in Europe these days, Hadriana dizzyingly incarnates the ideal of the femme-jardin that a local poet came up with long ago as a tribute to our Zaza.

Son of our beloved Priam Danoze, Hector, the chosen one, the most envied man in all of the Caribbean—does he have what it takes to care for the treasure that has been entrusted to him? That is the question this union raises for us all. Let us respond with a resounding yes. Admittedly, aside from his talents as an aviator and his attractive physical features, there is nothing superhuman that might distinguish the Danoze boy from any of Hadriana Siloé's other suitors. Up to this point, he has slain no dragons in this little city. But I, his godfather, have seen a quality grow within him that puts him head and shoulders above the other young men of his generation.

My godson's circle of loved ones extends well beyond his family, his fiancée, and his childhood friends. He has just as much love for the land of Jacmel, so often subjected to the weapons of fate: hurricanes, devastating fires, and Vlanbindingue spirits, not to mention the government scourges who chip away at the freedom of regular folks. Hector Danoze is as rooted in his passion for a woman as he is moved by the condition of his fellow townspeople.

In truth, after the misery of the last months, the marriage of these two exceptional beings is like a pact with hope and beauty that Jacmel will sign. All the love stories of the past, radiantly reanimated, will mingle freely in the immense blue skies of this wedding!

There was less of an epic tone and less lyricism in the announcement my family received:

Mr. and Mrs. André Siloé and Mr. and Mrs. Priam Danoze have the honour of announcing the marriage of their children Miss Hadriana Siloé and Mr. Hector Danoze. They graciously invite you to attend (or to join us in spirit for) the wedding Mass, which will take place on Saturday, January 29, 1938, at six in the evening, at the Saint Philippe and Saint Jacques Church. Father Yan Naélo will officiate. After the religious ceremony, Mrs. André Siloé and Mrs. Priam Danoze will host a reception at the Siloé manor, prior to the public festivities set to take place for the duration of the evening on Toussaint Louverture Square.

2

THE WEDDING PREPARATIONS made people forget about the hairdresser's sinister predictions. Scylla himself stopped talking about his oversexed protagonist and offered up his impressive talents to the committee of prominent citizens who were working twelve hours a day at city hall. Accompanied by a group of women, he feverishly ran up and down Seafront Street to gather monetary contributions from local businesses. In less than a week, the collection amounted to three times what the municipality usually managed to amass for celebrations of the patron saints, Philippe and Jacques.

The couple had registered at Nassaut's Little Gallery. Sébastien Nassaut, the owner, got things started by offering the betrothed a lavish Delft porcelain coffee set. Hundreds of other gifts were quickly purchased. There were so many presents that Scylla proposed loading them all into a small van, so that the whole community might bear witness to "the success of the future couple—the two H's of happiness (Hadriana and Hector)." He had heard about this custom from a traveller who had returned from a trip to Japan. Several days in a row, in the late morning or afternoon, Sébastien Nassaut used a bullhorn to invite people around town to applaud the basket of dreams that had been hitched to the festively beribboned vehicle. The traveling exhibition of gifts served as a kickoff to the night of feasting and extravagance everyone was awaiting.

Other ideas poured into the prefecture. Captain Gédéon Armantus, the chief of police, proposed a torchlight procession to open the festivities—leaving from the barracks on Burnt Widows Lane and making its way to the central square. Titus Paradou, official guide for the Brotherhood of the Magic Balls, let it be known that musicians and dancers from his famous carnival band would dispel any and all anxieties with their abundant exuberance and humour. Other carnival bands, among the most renowned in the region—like Madame Lil' Carême's Charles-Oscars, the Raras of Cochon-Gras, Pedro Curaçao's Bâtonnisses, the Ajax brothers' Tressés-Rubans, and the land surveyor Mathurin Lys's Mathurins—all promised to "offer this carnival of the century an incomparable hymn to the beauty of life and the freedom of love."

There were plans for the sacrifice of twenty-eight bulls, sixteen goats, thirty-three pigs, and an indeterminate number of poultry, to be served with a hundred bunches of plantains, sacks of rice and red beans, and dozens of kilos of sweet potatoes. They had also prepared thousands of codfish fritters, pastries, and various candies flavoured with coconut, ginger, and every other spice the archipelago had to offer. As for the drinks, there would be barrels of white rum, canisters and demijohns of ta a, rivers of Barbancourt, Veuve Cliquot, and French wines and liquors galore. Népomucène Homaire, an attorney in addition to his work at the newspaper, announced in the Southwest Gazette that he would be trying out an exceptionally strong punch he had made himself: no fewer than 365 different herbs had gone into the preparation. His great-grandfather Télamon Homaire had invented it during the hurricane of 1887, "to raise the spirits of all the male disaster victims who were left with their balls caught in a net."

All the artisans of Jacmel (dressmakers, tinsmiths,

shoemakers, basket weavers, coppersmiths) put their usual tasks on the back burner and devoted themselves to making masks and costumes for the carnival. City hall was stocked full with confetti and ribbons, boxes of streamers, pennants, garlands, and Venetian lanterns, for decorating the square. As for the mysterious unlabelled cardboard boxes that three firemen were seen unloading from a police truck, we assumed they contained fireworks and Bengal sparklers.

3

BACK IN THOSE days, I had a considerable advantage over Hadriana's other suitors: my mother, a well-respected milliner in Bel-Air, had been asked to make the bridal outfit. From dawn to dusk, her scissors and her Singer sewing machine offered a fabric serenade to the many charms of the young bride-to-be. All of us in Uncle Féfé's house floated along on an extraordinary cloud of tulle and silk, torrents of organdy and lace. As it emerged from my mother's virtuosic fingers, the bridal gown only deepened the fascinating mysteries of the flesh it would soon envelop.

At night, my mother would leave it on a mannequin. It was swathed entirely in tulle and superbly embroidered in a traditional style. The refinement of her sewing was singularly apparent in the transparency of the sleeves and the low-cut bodice accentuated with organdy and satin. Hanging in sensuous folds at the hips, the dress also boasted a huge bow at the back with a detachable false train. The real train, a cascade of lacy flounces, stretched out infinitely. The generous skirt, made for dancing and swishing about, seemed already to conceal within it the secrets of some sort of enchanted fan. The crown was decorated with interlacing silk threads and embossed with orange blossoms and iridescent sequins.

Once everyone had gone to bed at night, I would wake up without making a sound. My heart beating furiously, I would perform a passionate ritual in my mother's first-floor workshop. By the light of an oil lamp I brought with me, I danced with the mannequin. I caressed its curved neckline. I whispered words of tenderness to it with an intensity I myself barely understood. Fanning the flames of its power within the walls of our hearth, I sheltered it from the wind during those nights leading up to the fantastic voyage it was about to embark on with my beloved godsister.

By day, I skipped classes at school so I could watch Hadriana give herself over, body and soul, to her fittings. Though I had never paid much attention before, the familiar idea of a "fitting" began to expand like a balloon in my belly each time Hadriana, or Nana as she was often called, disrobed, without the slightest modesty, and slipped on that dress. She would pivot on her heels, arch her back, sway her hips, and square her shoulders, all with the utmost grace. The very next instant, dressed in all her bridal finery, she would hoist herself up onto a bench, bend a knee, raise an arm, thrust out her chest, and, without warning, sweep me up in a full English waltz. Perfectly following the instructions that my mother shouted through a mouth full of pins, Hadriana managed to make a celebration out of life's most tedious events. Looking at herself in the mirror, she would give her opinion, and finish by wrinkling her nose and sticking out her tongue at the ideal of French beauty that had set my young life on fire.

4

On Saturday, January 29, the bridal party left the Siloé manor at six in the evening. There were just over three hundred yards between there and the church. Arranged on either side of the church, a receiving line had been gathering since the late afternoon. A great clamouring of applause welcomed Hadriana as she moved forward on her father's arm.

"Long live the bride! Bravo, Nana!"

Flowers, confetti, streamers, and cries of admiration— "That's one hell of a beautiful girl!"—burst forth from everywhere at once. She approached the east side of the square—slender, sensual, and fluid in her white veils. Gloved to the elbows, she held a lace purse in one hand and a bouquet of assorted flowers in the other. Everything about her glowed, as if attempting to outshine the sun as it set over the bay. Entire families held their breath, feeling as if they were witnessing the most important sight of their lives. Several young girls I knew broke down weeping. One of them, my cousin Alina Oriol, swore to me thirty years later that the image that had been burned deepest into her memory was that of Hadriana as she took those first steps away from her home...

"I remember bursting into tears," she said.

"A sinister premonition?"

"Not at all. It was a much more complex emotion: to my eyes, her beauty was—for just a few moments—still linked to childhood dreams, to burning virginity, to amazing menstrual rhythms, to the gentle paternal hearth, to that freshness that marriage permanently takes from us women. More than any other young girl in Jacmel, Nana Siloé had a paradise to bury."

There on the church square, Hector Danoze, on my mother's arm, joined the procession as it moved solemnly through the nave toward the altar. The organs made the entire gaily decorated temple, filled to capacity, vibrate with the sparkling of thousands of candles.

The ceremony began under the direction of Father Naélo and two deacons, with the Saint Rose of Lima choir adding to the contagious excitement spreading throughout the crowd of attendees. Most of the faithful had gotten down on their knees to follow the service, assuming a posture of contemplation that reminded me of the intensity of Holy Week services. Awash in this radiant silence, we all sat or kneeled, anxiously poised to hear the wedding vows.

"Hector Danoze," said Father Naélo, "do you take Hadriana Siloé, present here before us, to be your lawfully wedded wife, according to the customs of our Holy Mother, the Church?"

"Yes, Father."

"Hadriana Siloé, do you take Hector Danoze, present here before us, to be your lawfully wedded husband, according to the customs of our Holy Mother, the Church?"

Hadriana let out a staggering "Yes" of distress and then immediately fell down at the feet of the priest. Dr. Sorapal rushed toward her. He held her wrist for what seemed like an eternity before crying out: "Hadriana Siloé is dead!"

Forty years later, the doctor's words still make me shudder. Hector Danoze and several others passed out immediately. People shouted questions in Creole with great cries of dismay.

Klariklé Philisbourg threw herself on the ground, tearing at her bridesmaid's dress. Mélissa Kraft, Olga Ximilien, Mimi Moravia, and Vanessa Lauture did the same. Father Naélo simply could not manage to calm them down. As the screams and general hysteria continued to drown out his voice, he climbed up the stairs of the pulpit.

"Silence, my dear brothers and sisters. Quiet down, I beg you. Hadriana Siloé has been taken from us at the very moment of her wedding. This scandal has occurred right here in her Father's house! Rather than give yourselves over to blasphemy, let us ask that He bestow His grace and mercy on the daughter He has struck down before us!"

"Grace and mercy!" cried hundreds of voices.

5

Maître Homaire lifted Hadriana from the altar's steps
where she was laid out and took her gently in his arms. Using
all his strength, he parted the agitated crowd like a breakwater.
At the exit to the church, those who had not been able to find
a place inside greeted them with cries of joy, thinking that this
was some kind of impromptu add-on to the ceremony. Amidst
the cheering of the crowd and the ringing of the bells, he
continued on toward the Siloé home, followed by a stampede
of people. Night had fallen. On the poorly lit edges of the
square, just about a hundred yards from his destination, yet
another misunderstanding awaited us.

"It's the newlyweds! Long live the newlyweds!"

With these cries, Titus Paradou's band of drummers and
musicians announced the beginning of the carnival of 1938
with a spirited dance of the *rabordaille*. Straight away, a group
of masked young men and women also began dancing in a
row, about two lengths ahead of the lawyer and the dead girl.
Holding one another by the waist and twisting their hips,
they transformed the deflated bridal party into a delirious
procession of joy leading all the way up to the doors of the
manor.

Maître Homaire placed the bride's body on a white sheet
spread out on the floor of the sitting room. From that moment
on, there began a pitiless battle between the two belief systems

that have long gone head-to-head in the Haitian imagination: Christianity and Vodou. Hadriana's parents soon began to lose control of the wake. The stately manor that had long presided high above the bay was transformed—in the blink of an eye—into a fantastical beehive: swarms of guests, most of them total strangers to the Siloés, freely began fussing over their deceased daughter. Without even asking their opinion, in the midst of the tears and lamentations, people rolled up the Persian rugs, moved the period furniture and the porcelain vases, covered the mirrors and the glass on the bronze clock with some white powdery substance, and turned over the seat cushions of the Louis XIV armchairs and sofa. Someone even had the idea to turn upside down a gorgeous English tea table inlaid with mosaic.

Once these preparations had been fully executed, one of the Siloés' neighbours, Madame Brévica Losange, reputed to be something of a *mambo*, suggested to the sobbing bridesmaids that they turn their panties and bras inside out and that they put their blouses and skirts on backward. She then declared loudly that Hadriana had not died of natural causes. And it certainly would not take Sherlock Holmes's talents to find the trail that would lead straight to the evildoer. This whole affair had Balthazar Granchiré's signature on it! With that, framed by the gilded panelling of the sitting room, she briefly recounted the same troubling facts that had been revealed to us in the square two months earlier by Scylla Syllabaire.

6

WERE THE SILOÉS actually expected to believe what they were hearing? In June of 1914, Hadriana's father had taken the entrance exam for École Polytechnique in Paris. Admitted with honours, he had been immediately snatched up by the Great War. At the end of this global battle, having taken up his studies again with equal success, André Siloé was all set to become a railroad engineer. But the sudden death of an uncle in Jacmel meant an obligation to take over the tobacco plant, which was the pride of the entire town. In March 1920, just a few days before leaving France, he married Denise Piroteau, an eighteen-year-old girl from Bordeaux, fresh out of the Saint Jeanne d'Arc Institute. She had had to give up the masters in classical literature she had begun at the Sorbonne in order to follow her husband to the Caribbean. Three years after Hadriana's death, André Siloé went off to Africa to join General de Gaulle's troops. Wounded at Bir Hakeim, he received a high-level decoration from General Kœnig himself. Colonel Siloé ultimately let himself die of sorrow in a hospital in Algiers, never having gotten over the loss of his beloved daughter. I met his widow several years later in the apartment she lived in on Raynouard Street in Paris. That day, I tried to jog her memory, hoping to learn what she and her husband had felt during those hours leading up to Hadriana's wake.

They had been deeply shocked to hear their neighbour cite

Nana's name in some scandalous story about a butterfly that preyed on young girls. Nevertheless, she and her husband had been too overcome with grief to react. Deep in their hearts, they had felt that this type of darkly salacious tale the woman had infused with so much fantasy was no doubt just part of the fictionalized lore that surrounded any Haitian funeral. At the end of the day, it was all just a question of the mysteries of death—our common fate. People from every background could certainly relate. She and André had long had that attitude—well before the tragedy that destroyed their happy home. As far as matters related to Vodou were concerned, they were far less prejudiced than the members of the Jacmelian elite they rubbed elbows with at the Excelsior Club. In this, they were not unlike the Danish exporter Henrik Radsen, an immensely curious individual who, following the path laid out by Jean Price-Mars, had initiated an invaluable research project on Haiti's national religion. Although very much practicing Catholics, she and André had found it perfectly natural that Hadriana's childhood be enriched by the incredible stories her black servants whispered to her as they performed their daily tasks or behind the closed doors of her bedroom. On the very night of her death, the Jacmelians who had loved and admired Hadriana like some kind of fairy princess integrated her into the vast repertoire of the country's folk imagination, in an utterly fantastic tale...

In fact, the state of total despondency into which the Siloés had both fallen immediately afterward kept them from ever being fully aware of the fierce battle over their child's body that was taking place under their own roof. At the time of this legendary wake, they looked like any old "white" couple, eternally dejected, condemned like any one of us to wander aimlessly among the sand dunes that the mysteries of Vodou

would swirl furiously around the spellbinding enigma that
was Hadriana Siloé's death.

7

THAT SAME NIGHT, so as to limit the damage as much as possible, my mother and a few others close to the Siloés spent their time trying to find some measure of compromise, however fragile, between the rites of Catholicism and those of Vodou, those two rivals fighting bitterly over the young girl's body and soul. But first, what was to be done about the crowd of merrymakers who had not stopped singing and dancing beneath the windows of the manor? Should they be permitted to encroach upon the solemnity of a Christian burial with the atmosphere of Caribbean revelry? For weeks, all anyone had been able to talk about was this one night of feasting and madness. Could they possibly be satisfied with a proper wake, a sombre affair conducted "in the manner of the French-from-France?" And then, also, should the bride's body be displayed? In the Siloés' sitting room, in the communal space of the town hall, or in the prefecture?

"Why not hold the viewing in the town square, under the hundred-year-old trees lining Lovers Lane?" suggested my uncle Ferdinand.

"That seems like an excellent idea to me," said Maître Homaire. "A virgin bride belongs to the realm of the stars and should be mourned beneath the open sky, near the nests of the birds... What do you two think?"

André and Denise Siloé nodded absentmindedly.

"Maître Homaire has just brought up the virginity of the deceased," interrupted Madame Losange. "In the case of a death like this one, isn't properly *deflowering* the victim the very first precaution to be taken? Who'll be handling that?"

Uncle Ferdinand tried delicately to evade the indelicate question. "That precaution would be absolutely useless in the case of a prominent French—and Catholic—family, thank the Lord," he argued.

"Prominent French family or not, registered Catholic back to front or not," insisted Madame Losange, "we've got to protect this child's final voyage. We could ask Lolita Philisbourg to do it, but I fear that the hand of a twin might further provoke the perversity of whatever evil genie is responsible for this death."

You could have cut the silence in that sitting room with a knife. The person standing closest to Madame Losange savagely pinched her fleshy thigh in an attempt to silence her, while my mother made discreet signs of disapproval.

"After all," she continued, undaunted, a fearsome gleam in her eye, "the sacred duty belongs to Hector Danoze, the legitimate spouse. But he's been hospitalized, left in a state of shock..."

"In my humble opinion," chimed in Scylla Syllabaire, "this task should be executed by an innocent. It should be done by a boy as virginal as the deceased."

"Do you have someone in mind?" asked Madame Losange.

"Why not Patrick Altamont?"

Completely stunned, I quickly lowered my head. Thankfully, my mother came to my rescue at once.

"Nana and Patrick were held over the baptismal fount by the same woman," she argued. "They're basically brother and sister. And I agree with Maître Homaire—the Siloé family is out of reach for the *bizangos*."

The minds of Hadriana's parents were elsewhere. They seemed to have gone back in time together, reliving their years with their cherished little French girl, a thousand miles from this profane discussion.

"It is my duty to insist," persisted the *mambo*. "Abominable violation threatens this angel we're shedding tears over right now. She must not arrive before God with her beautiful innocence sullied, her intimate self cruelly de led. It's the only thing missing from Granchiré's backlash. Believe Madame Brévica: the honeymoon of a *baka* is no First Communion party."

"To avoid it, all we have to do is place the lovely lady face-down," Togo Lafalaise, the tailor, remarked.

"No, not that, you fool," admonished Madame Losange. "Any *baka* kept from entering through a woman's garden side will head straight around to the backyard with an equally devastating erection! If we do away with the sacred *deflowering*, we must at the very least put a loaded pistol and a well-sharpened machete next to Miss Siloé. Athletic as she was, she'll be able to resist her abductors. We'll also need to sew up her mouth with black thread to keep her from answering when she hears her given name called out three times in the night."

This was the nature of the heated debate that was taking place when Reverend Father Naélo and his vicar, Father Maxitel, entered the sitting room. They headed straight for the sofa where Denise and André Siloé were seated. These four, along with my mother, my uncle Ferdinand, and Maître Homaire, sat for a long while and held a sort of private consultation to determine the details of the wake and the funeral. It was past eight o'clock when Father Naélo, looking worried, stood up and immediately began speaking.

"My dear friends," he said in a sermon-like tone, "Hadriana Siloé will be viewed underneath the silk-cotton trees in the town square in a manner that most conforms with our Christian traditions. Once Prefect Kraft has silenced the carnival, all Jacmel will get down on its knees and join in God's frontlines of defence to protect the remains of our dearly beloved fairy. After the formal Mass at noon, Madame Hector Danoze will be buried in accordance with the rites of our Sainted Mother, the Church. All together, in the dignity of our grief, we will be certain to respect the wishes of this honourable Catholic family that fate has so unjustly stricken in their adopted country. Madame Luc Altamont, creator of the bridal gown, is alone charged with dressing the body. We ask those who have nothing to add to this pious operation to please leave. In approximately one hour, we will all gather on the square. In truth, the whole world is disgraced when a young girl of nineteen is struck down on her wedding night."

"Amen," said all those present, crossing ourselves vigorously.

CHAPTER THREE

HADRIANA IN THE LAP OF THE GODS

Follow me to the bottom of that magic well that Jacmel
fell into that night, along with all its inhabitants.
—R.D.

1

LONG BEFORE THE clock struck ten p.m., Hadriana Siloé's catafalque had been placed between two rows of candles in the middle of Lovers Lane. The stars shone so low that they seemed part of the chapel. People had brought chairs and benches from all the nearby houses. When the open coffin arrived, all the carnival drums stopped at once. Not yet knowing what to do with my intense sadness, I took advantage of the sudden calm to slip into the crowd.

The carnivalesque bands had completely taken over every square meter of the plaza. As expected, the most prominent people of the southwest region were there. For the time being, musicians and dancers seemed to be bivouacked amongst their sleeping instruments: drums, *vaksin*, conch shells, rattles, saxophones, flutes, trumpets, and accordions. Dispersed here and there, eating and drinking under the trees, people began telling all those tales one tells at wakes.

I stopped first in front of a group of men dressed up as women. They had placed pillows and cushions under their green satin dresses, so as to simulate the final stages of pregnancy. They had the breasts and buttocks of the Venus Callipyge. Leaning on their clubs, the cross-dressers conversed with another group of revellers who, having wrapped themselves in white sheets and stuffed their ears and noses with cotton, spoke in decidedly nasal voices. A few steps away from these counterfeit-dead, a few half-naked werewolves, glazed from head to toe in cane syrup and soot, seemed to be plotting amongst themselves. The tin cones affixed to their fingertips clicked at the smallest of gestures. They had stuck orange peels between their teeth and lips, giving their faces terrifying expressions.

A little farther, I came upon Madame Lil' Carême's Charles-Oscars: adorned with blue and red kepis, they wore black fitted coats with saffron-yellow buttons, scarlet pants tucked into white gaiters, and giant spurs on their heels. Every Charles-Oscar boasted his military prowess with a sign hanging from his back: *Colonel Later-and-Sadder, Commander Who-Gives-Each-Household-Its-Share-of-Tribulations, Divisional-General-of-the-Seriously-Malicious-Member.*

Near the music kiosk, I came upon a school of Pierrots in multicoloured clothes, wearing pale-blue masks of metal cloth and bells on their belts. Alongside the police headquarters, Carib Indians, brilliant in their plumage, paid tribute to a demijohn of rum, their bows and arrows piled up on the sidewalk. Disguised as a vulture, the prefect's parrot General Télébec mockingly repeated: "Here's to you, you Indian pieces of shit!"

Camped out on the terrace of the Star Café were the Mathurins—that crew of devilish boys there to channel Jacmel's esteemed Mathurin Lys, the magical delegate who had fought long ago to put our dreams on the map. Clothed in loose bathrobes, they sported colourful papier-mâché Bolivar hats garnished with peacock feathers and long braids, and topped with assorted objects—horns, dolls, medallions, glass beads, small mirrors, amulets—all held together by a madras cloth and roped to a kind of bamboo mast.

Other masqueraders had set up camp on the eastern

72

and western edges of the square. Indian caciques frolicked freely with young Arawak beauties whose bare breasts rested harmoniously above brightly coloured pareos made of woven straw. Queen Elizabeth's pirate bands—the Brothers of the Coast and the Dogs of the Sea—had tattoos of skulls and snake vertebrae on their torsos. Under Francis Drake's tender gaze, they fearlessly felt up the sumptuous buttocks of Bambara African girls who wore nothing but flowered turbans, their pubis hidden by an elegant white velvet mask with phosphorescent lips and eyes.

Barons and marquesses of the court of Louis XIV played leapfrog on the lawn with friars in the habit of third-order Capuchins, rosaries on their belts, wooden crosses on their chests. High-ranking officers, black and mulatto, in the uniforms of the Grand Army of Napoleon, arm wrestled amicably with Marine Corps officers from the days when President Wilson's assault troops occupied our island.

In the colourful crowd I also recognized Simon Bolívar himself: completely and totally naked, he was engaged in an epic parry and thrust with the fervent and barbarous flesh of Pauline Bonaparte, while Toussaint Louverture, in the governor of Saint Domingue's uniform, jokingly pulled the ear of General Victor-Emmanuel Leclerc, the magnificently cuckolded husband of the future Princess of Borghese.

King Christophe, on an official visit to Versailles, paced majestically—arm in arm with the wife of Charles X—in front of mirrors that reflected sparkling images of a pleasure party to come. In a neighbouring salon, Alexandre Pétion, Mulatto and republican, was busy kissing the prodigiously lyrical thighs of the very young Madame Récamier with a passion equal to that of the other Alexander, the Macedonian general.

A few feet away, the Haitian emperor Jacques the

First played some form of table tennis with his partner, Generalissimo Stalin. Joseph Vissarionovich Dzhugashvili was decked out in the formal costume worn by all Russian czars. Those two petite fathers of their people showed equal dexterity as they volleyed a human head back and forth, the head having been shrunken using a technique invented by the Jivaros. This primitive ping-pong ball changed from black to white to yellow to red in accordance with whichever world championship was being disputed.

All over the square, the various masks reconstituted the particular time and space that corresponded with the heroes they represented at the moment of their participation in the planet's history. But historical memory had gotten mixed up to the point of ridiculousness, not unlike the paths that once led people from the capital to the Tarpeian Rock. Alongside all the legendary characters, but never truly joining them in their fantastic adventure, roamed a host of other Jacmelian visions, just as fancifully dressed, but who had opted for the less spectacular roles of pigs, orangutans, birds of prey, bulls, sharks, cobras, crocodiles, tigers, Tonton-Macoutes, and leopards.

This masked occasion had convoked three centuries of human history to my sister's wake. Figures sculpted from the purest marble and figurines of rotten wood had come together to dance, sing, drink rum, and refuse death, kicking up the dust on my village square, which, in the midst of this general masquerade, took itself for the cosmic stage of the universe.

2

WHILE I WAS gone, Hadriana's parents had taken up their position next to the catafalque. They were flanked by the most prominent citizens of Jacmel. I identified many familiar faces. Madame Brévica Losange seemed to have completely recovered from her disappointment of earlier that evening. Having gone home to change, she was back looking fresh as day in a long indigo dress—reminiscent of those *caraco* tunics of days past—that draped without a wrinkle over her laced boots. She had gathered her gray hair on the nape of her neck in an impeccable 1900-style bun. It was said later that the necklace she wore on her bosom had a spirit imprisoned in each of its amber beads. A subsequent calculation led to the conclusion that no less than three dozen spirits kept company with Madame Brévica's highly perched breasts during the long nocturnal march of January 29–30, 1938.

When I arrived, I noticed a tension among those gathered that seemed not to be connected to mourning, no matter how intensely everyone was grieving for Nana. Seeing my confusion, my mother rushed to quietly fill me in on what had happened during the previous hour.

"Everything has been set," she whispered to me. "The prefect has already decided: the festivities will take place as planned."

"With drums, dancing, and everything?"

"Yes. The priests and nuns, supported by a few zealots, failed to get the authorities to postpone carnival simply because of Nana's death."

"How did they try to make their case?"

"Father Naélo said that an explosion of paganism on the square risked forever compromising *the salvation of the angel of love Jacmel was mourning.*"

"And what else, tell me!"

"Cécilia Ramonet said that the carnival groups would not be satisfied with dancing and singing modestly in homage to Hadriana. We had to be prepared for all the orgiastic excesses of Vodou."

"Such as?"

"Animal sacrifices, lascivious dances, a red Sabbath, and other scenes of witchcraft."

"Who was in the other camp?"

"Maître Homaire, Uncle Féfé, doctors Braget and Sorapal, Didi Brifas, and Lil' Jérôme Villaret-Joyeuse—and me too, of course."

"What did Maître Homaire say?"

"*Nana Siloé must remain forever linked in our town's memory to the passion for life that burned within her more radiantly than in any young woman of her generation.*"

"He actually said that?"

"*Her beauty*, he added, *resounded far more like the beating of a drum than the tolling of a bell!*"

"And the priests had nothing to say to that?"

"Father Maxitel said that such declarations amounted to Freemasonry. Sister Hortense said Maître Homaire should be ashamed of having profaned the open coffin of a saint in the presence of her intercessors before God."

"Didn't Dr. Braget say anything?"

"He went even further. He said that the *banda* dance, when performed with real talent, was the most beautiful form of prayer that men and women had ever invented."

"Fuel to the fire!"

"Wait, it gets better!"

"Impossible. Okay, go ahead."

"Henrik Radsen, in all his blustering Danishness, stepped up. He said that, even more so than prayers, the dances of Vodou were unparalleled hymns to the human adventure that God keeps rolling out like a carpet under our feet here in this world. *In Europe,* he said, *the faithful pray using their eyes, hands, knees, and lips. Haiti's charm in its dealings with God is that the hips, loins, buttocks, and private parts all take part in the soul's most exalted deeds. They are the very driving force of redemption. The banda is perhaps the most beautiful oratorical form ever imagined.*"

With these words, Mam Diani told me, the priests and nuns made the sign of the cross, speechless with indignation. Sister Hortense threw herself to her knees, both hands on her rosary.

"Then," my mother continued, "Cécilia Ramonet, even more of a hard-nosed widow than ever, went on the attack. *Sirs,* she said, *you're going to end up killing the Siloés' wonderchild a second time. It isn't enough that she's dead—you want to add the bestial rutting of Baron-Samedi! Isn't the brutality of her disappearance enough for you? Now you want to deliver her to the tribe of pagan gods who debase this Christian country!*"

"I certainly hope you protested," I said to my mother.

"My blood was boiling. I don't know where I got the courage to confront General César in public! *I was with Nana for every step of her short life,* I said. *Before making her wedding gown, I'd already sewn her the first dress she ever wore. I made sure that her godmother, Germaine Muzac, was also godmother to my only son. I saw her transform from a little tyke into an exceptional beauty. She wouldn't have appreciated what you just said. The only time I ever heard her talk about death, do you know what she said to me? 'If I die young, I would like my death to be lived by all those who loved me—lived through the drums and masks of a carnival celebration!'"*

I wanted to throw my arms around my mother's neck to thank her. She had not betrayed the girl of my dreams!

"Who spoke after you?"

"None other than the prefect, Barnabé Kraft. *I haven't said anything until now,* he said, *because I wanted to give everyone a chance to speak their mind. Here's my opinion as prefect: the party shall proceed as planned. I've consulted with the Siloés and the Danozes: André and Denise, Priam and Carmita, like myself, would like for there to be no changes in the unfolding of the festivities Jacmel had planned for the celebration of their children's happiness."*

3

AT THAT VERY moment, the bugle for the torchlight procession
sounded on the north corner of the plaza. Captain Armantus's
men burst onto the square. As they approached the crowd,
they began marching in step. Bare-chested, torches aloft,
they were all dressed up in the garb of François Makandal's
infamous turban-wearing Maroons. Spurred on by the bugles,
the carnival musicians all of a sudden called upon the libertine
spirits of the *rada* drums. Vodou immediately took over the
military march, the way a flaming cock drowns out the squawks
of a runaway hen. Straight away, the Maroon impersonators
and the various masked people on the square gave themselves
up to an extraordinary dance of shoulders and hips, their knees
slightly bent, their heads and torsos vigorously thrust forward.
Hundreds of people began pivoting on themselves, never
interrupting the feverish rotation of their hips. Others hopped
on one foot, pretended to kneel down, then began leaping and
spinning in wild abandon, as agile as any feline. About thirty
yards from the catafalque, the musicians suddenly cut short
the frenzy by executing a perfectly timed drum break: the
crowd stopped dancing and began imitating Hadriana Siloé's
stiffened corpse, transforming the square into a region of the
kingdom of the dead.

Captain Armantus approached the chapel alone. He
lowered his torch over the coffin, right over Hadriana's face.

His ear cocked, he seemed to be listening to something terribly sad. He hung on the dead girl's words, drinking in something clearly very crucial. He then lifted his right arm to offer a military salute. But instead of finishing the gesture, he let loose a scream that was like nothing anyone had ever heard—aside, of course, from the one we had heard a few hours earlier under the vault of the church. He began walking backward until he reached the policemen at the rear of the gathering. He then spoke in a low voice to the bugle players, who quickly sounded the death knell. Immediately afterward, Captain Armantus ordered his men to make an about-face before hustling them back to the barracks at top speed.

4

AMONG ALL THE mysteries that would end up defying our
common sense that year, Armantus's behaviour remained one
of the most disconcerting. Several witnesses tried in vain to
figure out what had happened. But the serviceman chose to
leave the police, Jacmel, and the country rather than share
with anyone even the smallest detail regarding his panicked
reaction to Hadriana Siloé's mortal remains.

I realize this is going to sound incredible, but what follows
is a true story. Feel free not to believe me. One afternoon in
the winter of 1955, in New York City, I hailed a taxi just in
front of the Pennsylvania Hotel, intending to visit the Statue
of Liberty. The driver and I immediately felt a connection. He
asked me in English what my nationality was. I'm not sure
why, but I got the idea in my head to hide the fact that I was
Haitian. Randomly, I told him I was from Dahomey. My lie
had the most surprising effect on him.

"You said Da-ho-mey, right? The country where the Port
of Ouidah is?"

"Exactly."

"What day is it today?"

"Friday, November 18."

"You said Friday, right?" the taxi driver pressed.

"Yes, indeed. Yesterday was Thursday and tomorrow
Saturday."

"So to be clear: on Friday, November 18, in the year of our Lord 1955, a citizen of Dahomey jumped into the taxi of the former Captain Gédéon Armantus. Destination: the Statue of Liberty, in New York City! Have I got that right?"

"What's so extraordinary about that?" I asked, profoundly taken aback.

"Why everything, my dear sir! I have been awaiting this miracle for the last eighteen years! An encounter with a messenger from Ouidah, a Friday, the eighteenth of November—all three elements converging at once just as my Aunt Euphémie predicted!"

"Aunt Euphémie?"

"My great-aunt who died in the early 1930s. She appeared before me in 1938 in the coffin of a young French girl who'd died on the night of her wedding, at the very height of her physical glory!"

"Forget the Statue of Liberty," I told him, overwhelmed. "Drive wherever you want, no matter what it costs. Tell me everything."

And so it was that I was given the key to Gédéon Armantus's crack-up on the night of January 29, 1938—and from the man himself! Leaning over Hadriana's open coffin, his hand already reaching up to perform a respectful military salute, he had discovered that the lovely face familiar to all of Jacmel had been replaced, to his great astonishment, with the mummified visage of his old aunt, deceased five years earlier at the age of 107 after having taught civics for half a century at the Célie-Lamour School for Young Girls. Apparently, the former schoolteacher had whispered to him: "My darling nephew, do something for me: do not leave here without having your bugles sound a death knell for all to hear. Some of humanity's very greatest lie in rest right here under Toussaint

HADRIANA IN ALL MY DREAMS

Louverture Square!"

Two days later, when her spirit was contacted through a *loa*, Aunt Euphémie confirmed what she had said at Hadriana's funeral. She made her descendant swear, on pain of death, never to tell anyone the secret she had entrusted to him, "unless," she said, "you cross paths—preferably in New York, among the white Americans—on a Friday, November 18, anniversary of the victory of the Haitian army at Vertières, with a man from the land of Ouidah, Dahomey. To him alone are you permitted to relay the message that might otherwise cause a serious aneurysm in your Jacmelian brain!"

5

CAPTAIN ARMANTUS'S BUGLE call had, in effect, driven Jacmel to the edge of a collective embolism. An impenetrable congestion of red blood cells hung over the square, provoking a general existential weightlessness: for several minutes we experienced the same malaise that a pod of dolphins must experience when washed up on a sunny beach. We could each hear our own panting breath, our own heart pounding to beat the band, as well as that of the person next to us. Seated near Maître Homaire, I could distinctly hear the pileup of all sorts of metaphors rippling in that exceedingly creative man's formidable brain! What saved us from a collective thrombosis was the stabbing of a young pig that some clever Jacmelian had the presence of mind to initiate at that very instant; the shrill cries of the near-decapitated animal pulled the crowd out of its death throes. The drums of a new *banda*, even more feverish than the one that had come before, reinfused everyone's blood with the very strongest beats of life.

6

WITHOUT LOSING ANY time, Madame Brévica Losange jumped with both feet into the role for which she had probably been born, early one morning in April 1894, in southwest Haiti. She peered into a woven bag, out of which she solemnly extracted the elements of a costume: a tricornered hat, a red military shirt, a purple cardboard mask of a Catholic saint, two small bags, a bottle, a pair of driving gloves and goggles from the year 1900, a short, thick black candle, and a bundle of pine.

"What's she doing?" I asked my mother.

"She's preparing an *expédition* against the evil spirits of death. It's a well-known conjuring rite."

Madame Losange put on the grenadier's blouse, placed the patent-leather tricornered hat on her head, and slipped on the driving gloves. Once she had secured the mask and glasses on her face, she took a few steps toward the catafalque and greeted the Siloé family with a graceful bow, her chest pressing forward. She uncorked the bottle and spread a few drops of its pinkish contents to the right and left, just in front of the catafalque, while chanting, *Apo lisa gbadia tâmerra dabô!* Then she raised the bottle in a salute to the cardinal points of the square and quickly tilted its neck over Hadriana's face. With these ceremonial libations complete, she kissed the polished wood of the coffin three times, poured some ashes into her right hand, and drew three circles, topped with a cross, on the ground right in front of the catafalque. She emptied another of her little bags and used coffee grounds to trace the contours of a giant butterfly, his wings outstretched over female genitalia.

"What do you see?" I asked my mother.

"Some kind of strangely patterned zodiac!"

7

THERE BEFORE OUR eyes, the talented Madame Brévica had sketched a monstrous halfbreed creature lusting after a beautifully shaped solar-vulva, its lips and clitoris spread wide open. She picked up a few sticks of pine and started a fire. We watched her every move with rapt attention. All the good Christian folk had their heads bowed in prayer as they recited the Rosary with desperate piety. The Siloés, their thoughts elsewhere, were busy unwinding interior Rosary beads, unfamiliar to us blacks. Jacmel's good Catholic families—the Fontants, Ramonets, Voucards, Zitals, Douzets—seemed crushed beneath a double sense of shame: first, the blasphemous display of African customs; and second, the aggressive desecration of white flesh.

Madame Losange suddenly called everyone's attention to the steps of the funeral rite over which she was presiding. "Hellfire and damnation," she shouted. "The flames of redemption demand to be fed!"

With that, several of the onlookers began feeding the fire. One person started things off by throwing in some old copies of the *Southwest Gazette*. Upon seeing the flames flare up, Lolita Philisbourg took off her bra and fed it to the fire. Her sister Klariklé watched her sibling's offering and upped the ante, tossing in her Italian-made garter belt. Mélissa Kraft and some of the other young girls gave up their silk stockings and satin lingerie. The men threw in socks, ties, and handkerchiefs. A few of the disabled gave up a crutch here, a mahogany arm there. A straw hat, a mask of Pope Alexander Borgia, an umbrella, a small bench, a rattan chair, an enormous Gothic dildo, and a nun's wimple all landed in the increasingly robust flames. Madame Losange's face tensed with pleasure as she contemplated the joyful erection of the blaze. She took one of the burning twenty-pound candles next to the catafalque and planted it above the drawing of the dead girl's genitals, thus attempting to thwart the butterfly's rapacious intentions. Madame Brévica raised her voice once more, this time to ask that the celebration's three principle drummers—Fat Cyclone, Master Timebal, and General Lil' Congo—be brought to her side.

"Princes of the *rada* rhythm," she said while pouring out rum for them to drink, "join this battle to protect the final rest of the princess lying here before us!"

From the very first steps of the dance, Saint Jacques the Major, leader of the Ogoun family of warrior spirits, took possession of Madame Brévica Losange. As soon as she had been "mounted" by the spirit, the *mambo* began improvising a song to the rhythm of the drums.

> *Loa Saint Jacques, patron saint of Jacmel,*
> *Protect our beautiful Nana.*
> *A cursed butterfly has bewitched her.*
> *You who so adore the solar-vagina,*
> *Bring it back to life in our blood!*
>
> *Loa Saint Jacques, General of the Fire,*
> *With your love for big tits,*
> *Reignite Nana Siloé in our lives!*

Once the crowd picked up the melody and the words, the whole wake exploded. No one could pray on his or her knees any longer. Everyone was seized by a violent urge to sing, dance, and shout—to roar in the face of death's sacred visage. With their Christian idea of mortality deeply offended, the clergy discretely disappeared—first the two parish priests, then the director and the Mother Superior of the two congregational schools, and then the monks and nuns. After their departure, no great wind of vice began blowing over the square, as often was claimed in the days and months that followed. Everything took place within the bounds of a pagan tribute to Hadriana Siloé. At no point—not even when the Enchanted Balls entered on the scene—did her final celebration threaten to become some sort of priapic occult ceremony, a Caribbean Walpurgis Night, or the unbridled Saturnalia of a scandalous Haitian-style masked ball! On the contrary, the drums, *vaksin*, and wind instruments transformed Madame Losange's song into the brightest of nights: their musical fury carried each of us back and forth between death and birth, between anguished screams and triumphant orgasmic cries. The musical volcano reduced the legendary obstacles between Thanatos and Eros to ashes, went beyond any prohibitions separating the sperm of black men from the ovaries of white women. The explosion of *guédé* spirits, enlivened by our seething blood, placed our bodies and souls, our frenzied penises and vaginas, into a space of cosmic harmony, fuelled by the crazy hope that we might somehow snatch Nana Siloé back from death so that the radiance of her earthly being might shine in our lives once again.

That senseless hope electrified the crowd. Beyond Madame Losange, numerous other people became vessels for the gods. Among the possessed who had been mounted by spirits ranging from Agoué Taroyo and Damballah-Ouèdo to Baron-Samedi and many others, a black woman of about twenty years old stood out. Her face was protected by a mask, nicely adorned with a lace veil, which she wore beneath a large feathered hat like those in Mexican engravings. She was clothed only in a diaphanous garment of embroidered tulle. The *mambo* signalled to her to approach the fire. She whispered something in her ear. People on the square were saying that the goddess Erzili, guardian of the freshest and clearest waters, and protector of life's infinite enchantments, had possessed the unknown woman.

"Who do you think that is?" I asked my mother.

"I have no idea who it could be. But she's certainly a beautiful wisp of a girl! As for the spirit, I recognize her: she's a Spanish goddess, the Black Virgin of Altagracia. She comes from Hatuey, in the Dominican Republic. In addition to Erzili, she's often called Fréda Toucan-Dahomin. She's one of the good ones, venerated on both sides of the border. She's also worshipped in Cuba and Brazil. Fréda watches over honeymoons and all other acts of love!"

The dazzling Fréda came upon the erotic drawing that had been sketched at the foot of the catafalque. She seemed to recognize it as the genital light shining in herself. She saluted it respectfully. Then, at some distance from the other spirits, Madame Losange and Fréda began undulating their shoulders and feet, performing feints, leaps, and rapid turns, as if transported by the ebb and flow of an invisible wave. Saint Jacques the Major (Brévica) danced like a master. But all eyes were on the young girl in the wedding veil, her beauty and grace matched only by that of the deceased. Her dancing of the *yanvalou-dos-bas* was marked by an astonishing sensuality: under the transparent veil, her naked curves resembled the swaying path of some imaginary boat. She stopped dancing around the flames, took off her veil, and pretended to set it on fire. Then she drew it around her neck, over her breasts, across her buttocks, and between her thighs, like a foamy sponge of salvation. Once she had completed her sacred ablutions, she put the veil back on but kept it lifted up to her hips so as to join Saint Jacques the Major in miming the pelvic thrusts of a phenomenal sex act.

8

Titus Paradou chose the exact moment of this symbolic copulation to launch the parade of his famous Brotherhood of the Magic Balls. Heads protruding, necks stiff, the group of young people held each other by the waist and, rotating their hips, advanced in a single file behind their leader, feet abandoned to the rhythm of a *nago-grand-coup*. The contagious music put the whole square back in motion. Along all of its paths, rows of men and women, most of them masked (as historical personalities, notably), rolled their torsos while taking short, compressed steps, shaking their shoulders and hips as if trying to dislocate every bone in their bodies. These masked revellers were soon joined by the dignitaries and by all those who, for fear of offending the quiet suffering of the Siloés, had not dared leave their chairs, confined to their roles as spectators. My mother and I, along with Maître Homaire, Henrik Radsen, the Philisbourg twins, the Kraft sisters, my uncle Féfé, and many others, gave in to the desire to join the dancing anthill.

Led by Titus Paradou, Madame Brévica, and Erzili, the chain of dancers circled the catafalque seven times. As they danced alongside the open coffin, everyone got the chance to say a personal farewell to the young woman. The general feeling—which was much commented on subsequently—was that death had not altered her features in the slightest. She looked to be sleeping peacefully, her eyes lightly closed and her mouth traversed by a kind of ineffable joy. It was, as Maître Homaire would later put it, "the smile of a being grappling only with the mystery of her interrupted dream of love."

Among the impassioned commentaries incited by the lawyer's article, there were several bizarrely framed comparisons of Hadriana's smile to Mona Lisa's famous grin. Maître Homaire, among others, had written:

> In the bluish veil of the early morning, which seemed itself to have fused with her wedding veil, the sense of sublunary enchantment that emanated from Hadriana Siloé's death was heightened measurably by the enigmatic joy that graced her lips. As with the Mona Lisa, the charms of her face seemed to have turned inward, completely cleansed of the troubling circumstances of her death and wondrously instilled with the inner incandescence that is the mark of eternal feminine beauty.

When I arrived in Paris in late 1946, I breathlessly rushed to the Louvre—to Leonardo's famous canvas—as if this were to be my first rendezvous, far from Jacmel, with Nana Siloé. I found myself profoundly disappointed. The *Mona Lisa* was certainly the masterpiece of a true genius, but compared to the young girl of my memories, she seemed to be sneering, without the slightest bit of inner passion. Frozen within the frame of my incurable nostalgia, Hadriana's wedding makeup was still intact; the skin of her neck and hands was as smooth and fresh as a mango picked just before sunrise. Death had given her beauty a look of joyous profundity, as if she had been captivated from within by a dream more extraordinary than life and death put together. The curve of her lips looked like no other smile, however renowned. It was a fruit bursting with freshness that any eager mouth would have longed to bite to the point of ecstasy.

9

THE LIGHT AT six o'clock on Sunday, January 30 had painted the trees on the square in monochromatic shades. Titus Paradou's farandole had brought the night to its climax. All there was left to do before the funeral was burn the Papa Mardi Gras. *Would everything be forgiven?* the crowd wondered. The Philisbourg twins gave the answer. They presented one of the greatest surprises of the wake, arriving unexpectedly with the effigy of an enormous butterfly. Everyone realized that someone important had been left out of the celebration: Balthazar Granchiré. We all stopped singing and dancing immediately. The fire was dying out, so people began once again tossing in old newspapers, false breasts, polished tricornered hats, panties and underwear, and a few fistfuls of sea salt.

The ceremony nearly took a bad turn: a young man whose engagement had been broken off because of the butterfly fired a pistol at its likeness. The bullet got caught in the puppet's stuffing less than an inch from Lolita Philisbourg's left breast. With lightning speed, Fréda Toucan-Dahomin used a machete to symbolically cut off the butterfly's erect penis. Once castrated, he was thrown into the blaze. He burst into flames amidst a solemn silence. Someone shouted: "Down with Granchiré! Nana is resurrected!"

As if in echo to that cry of hope, the tolling of the first bells announced the funeral. Fathers Naélo and Maxitel appeared, preceded by a crucifer. Forcefully, they cleared a path in the direction of the chapel. The raising of the body was imminent. The two dancers had just enough time to dip their thumbs into the Papa Mardi Gras's burning ashes. In the presence of the two priests, each woman traced the sign of the cross on Hadriana Siloé's forehead. The celebration slowly died out, and we all made an effort to regain our composure while still caught up in the uninhibited merriment of the previous hours.

CHAPTER FOUR
Requiem for a Creole Fairy

Death and Beauty are two things so profound,
So of dark and azure, that one might say that
They were two sisters terrible and fecund
Possessing the one enigma, the one secret.
—Victor Hugo

1

DESPITE THE SHORT distance separating the church from the town square, we were completely out of breath when we arrived just behind the casket. The joyful decorations of the holy site were unchanged. Father Naélo had not had the brightly coloured wedding banner replaced by the wall hangings appropriate for mourning. One might have believed even that the ceremony was going to pick up where it had left off the night before.

After the Kyrie Eleison had been sung by the nuns, and the words of the Book of Wisdom and the Gospel According to Saint Jean read by Father Maxitel, Father Naélo's homily brought us abruptly back to the real world.

"Hadriana was her saintly Christian name," the priest began. "Instead of the Christian wake her purity deserved, Jacmel has subjected her to the outrageousness of a night of carnival. To the injustice of her death has been added the scandal of masks and the most unbridled pagan dances.

"The fact is this: by enacting this unseemly ritual, Jacmel has sullied the innocence of its fairy. In truth, my dear brothers and sisters, Hadriana had no need of help from our *guédé* spirits, nor did she need the accompaniment of our drums or our obscene and macabre dances in order to appear before her true God. These impious undertakings have greatly degraded her passing.

"In this horrible January, here in Haiti, dear Lord, we beg Your forgiveness for all those who have soiled the virginal morning of Your beloved flower. We ask—on behalf of Hadriana and all of Jacmel, as it grieves for its angel—for the mercy of the Father, the Son, and the Holy Spirit!

"The radiant young woman before us had an exceptional gift for being present in the world, Lord. Let the waters of your mercy run cool and clear on her naked feet as she makes her harsh ascendance toward the assembly of saints over whom you preside in your heavenly kingdom!

"Yes, Christ the Redeemer, receive Hadriana as a sentry awaits the first light! Take no offense at these Vodou ministrations and forgive Your little town of Jacmel. These Jacmelians love You above all else, and their love has hope for Madame Hector Danoze, in all honour and in all glory!

> *"Lord we pray for Your servant*
> *the Creole fairy, Hadriana Siloé,*
> *we pray for her star*
> *that has shone but once!*
>
> *"Saint Mary, mother of God,*
> *pray for the poor sinners of Jacmel,*
> *now and at the hour of their death*
> *deliver us from the masks*
> *and the drums of paganism.*

"In memory of the baptism that this regal body received here in this very place, in the house of her Father, and in which she died at age nineteen; in memory of her radiant beauty; in memory of her radiant soul, bluer than all the blue of the sky, Lord, beyond the pain and the tears, may Your beneficent smile welcome her at the doors of heaven! Farewell, madame!"

At the end of these funeral rites, the chorus of nuns heaped a few Latin phrases upon the grief-stricken Caribbean, on this, its first Sunday without Nana Siloé. The faces of those good people still wearing their masks now appeared to my confused eyes as tiny coconut-shell lamps filled with castor oil.

"*Accende lumen sensibus, infunde amorem cordibus, in rma nostril corporis, virtute firmans perpeti... De Profundis... Dies irae, dies illa... Libera me... Dona eis requiem... in paradiso...*"

2

FOR THE SECOND time in less than twenty-four hours, Haitian arms carried Hadriana hurriedly out of the church of her childhood. At the exit, the smoky *tête-gridape* lamps flapped their owls' wings in the bright morning sunshine. Hundreds of people, crushed to the bone with fatigue, had returned home once the party had died down. The number of those who accompanied Nana to the end was nevertheless very impressive. The convoy marched off at a good pace behind the crucifer, in a tide of flowers. From the temple to the cemetery, there was not more than a mile to walk. About a hundred yards from the entry gate there was a little hill to climb. It was well known to frequent funeral-goers by the name of "Melpomène Saint Amant's pubis." It was there that the convoy suddenly reared up like a spooked horse. A man who looked a lot like Baron-Samedi invited some of the *guédés* present to take the coffin from the hands of its apostolic bearers. These Vodou gods of death immediately began to sing and dance. They staggered forward then back with the coffin, making a series of shifts and sudden about-turns, such that the whole of the funeral procession was obliged to do the same. They repeated this exercise three times around the perimeter of that erotic hill before deciding to run across it at top speed.

"What are they doing?" I asked my uncle Féfé.

"The gods are trying to disorient Nana's innermost self—

her *petit bon ange*. Should it ever get the idea to head back home, it won't be able to find its way."

3

IN THE MAIN path of the cemetery, Prefect Kraft, Henrik Radsen, Maître Homaire, and my uncle Ferdinand took over for the *guédés*. We were still a decent distance from the grave site. Not having a family vault in Jacmel, the Siloés had obtained a plot that looked out over the length of the entire bay. The gravediggers were waiting in the shade of an almond tree, but upon seeing the masked figures dispersed throughout the cemetery and headed their way, they nearly hightailed it out of there. We all gathered around Hadriana's parents. Father Naélo took the holy water presented to him by a choirboy. Solemnly, he sprinkled it on the casket, which lay on the ground atop the heaps of dirt piled up alongside the grave. Was someone going to say a few words? The pallbearers were getting ready to wrap the rope around the coffin when Maître Homaire signalled for them to wait. Someone handed him a long black case. He took out a flute that all his neighbours knew well and began to play a regal melody. Although the tune was not well known in Jacmel, it nevertheless made quite an impact. Everyone was crying, Catholics and Vodouists alike. Years later in Milan, at La Scala, I learned that it was a piece from *Nabucco* by Giuseppe Verdi: the choral music of the Hebrew captives, "*Va, pensiero!*" Maître Homaire then went on to play "Sorrowful Sunday," a very popular song at the time, which people said had inspired lovelorn souls across the world to commit suicide. The words were on everyone's lips, and the crowd readily sang along with the flautist:

> *"I will die one Sunday from having suffered too much.*
> *Then you'll come back but I will have left.*
> *Candles will burn tenderly like hope*
> *For you, only for you, my eyes will be open.*
> *Don't fear my eyes, even if they can't see you,*
> *They will tell you that I loved you more than life.*
> *On that dark Sunday, my arms filled with flowers,*
> *I stayed all alone in my little room*
> *Where, alas, I knew you'd never come.*
> *I murmured words of love and heartache,*
> *I stayed all alone and cried softly,*
> *Listening to the cold December wind,*
>
> *Sorrowful Sunday!"*

* * *

On that splendid Jacmelian Sunday, the song had a most unexpected effect. Joy shone through the tears in everyone's eyes. The jubilant sounds of the sun-filled morning overwhelmed the burial—a cock flirting with three hens at once in a neighbouring banana plantation, a young couple riding bareback on a roan horse as it galloped through two red hedges and an arbour of daisies, birds chasing each other wildly through the branches of an almond tree swaying in the sea breeze. On that glorious day in Haiti, endlessly and immensely blue, all sadness melted into the extraordinary azure of the bay. Grief did not really suit our farewells. Even the mere sound of stones on the wood coffin would resonate in our memories for years afterward like an echo of life that was somehow greater than our sorrow.

4

On Monday, January 31, I hurried home right after finishing my morning class at Pinchinat High School. Mam Diani, my uncle Féfé, and his wife, Auntie Émilie, were in a heated discussion in the atelier. None of them could keep still; they all had cups of "fainting tea" in their hands. Without giving me a chance to speak, my mother handed one to me.

"Now what's happened?" I asked after taking a sip.

"Patrick, please have another sip," said my mother. "Féfé has just come back from the Siloé manor: Nana has disappeared from her grave!"

"What?!" I replied, stupefied, addressing my uncle.

Apparently, one of the gravediggers had returned to the burial site looking for a shovel he had left behind, only to find the grave empty. Scared nearly to death, he made a beeline for the rectory. Father Naélo had listened carefully, and between the gravedigger's panting and stuttering, the good Father managed to extract the following piece of information: "In the place of the beautiful bride, buried right here in front of everyone, there's nothing left but a jug of rainwater, its contents evaporating in the heat of the sun!"

The priest immediately alerted the authorities. My uncle, the magistrate, Prefect Kraft, Captain Cayot (standing in for the bedridden Captain Armantus), Dr. Sorapal, the medical examiner, and Maître Homaire (on behalf of the press) had all accompanied the priest to the cemetery. Underneath the almond tree where Madame Hector Danoze had been buried just the night before, they found a gaping hole with nothing in it aside from a tiny puddle of water left over from a recent downpour. The body, the coffin, the flowers—everything had vanished into thin air!

At the request of the prefect, my uncle immediately wrote up a statement describing the scene. In compliance with Article 246 of the existing penal code, a legal dossier would be opened officially against X for having flagrantly desecrated the young bride's grave, for having taken her *petit bon ange* hostage during her wedding ceremony, and for the criminal sequestration of her reanimated body.

In a state of complete agitation, the officials then went together to the Siloés' home. The prefect explained to them that at some point between Sunday night and Monday morning, their daughter had been the victim of what was likely some sort of ritualistic crime—she had been raised from her grave and forcibly taken to an unknown destination.

Hadriana's parents received both the news and Father Naélo's uncomfortable explanations with looks that were at once incredulous and resigned. After what they had been through since Saturday's events, nothing really could have shocked them any further. It was all perfectly clear to them— at both Hadriana's wake and funeral, in the moving tribute to her beauty—that the "real" Haiti had been exposed. Incapable of accepting that a heart attack had toppled Nana at the foot of the altar, the Jacmelians—with their necrophilic imagination—had incorporated their daughter into some sort of fairy tale. The disappearance of her body from the grave was the final episode in this leap into an imaginary world that was straining to grapple with fear and death. It was the tribute that their misfortune was obliged to pay to the magical identity of their adopted country.

"Denise and I," André Siloé had concluded, "like you—like you, sirs, or, in fact, like you, Reverend Father—we can do nothing to fight the complex web of fables and fiction that surround the fatefulness of death and life in Haiti. In order to deal with that double inevitability, Christ himself (if ever he let himself get mixed up in Haitian affairs) would be as armless as the *Venus de Milo*."

"He said all of that with humour and an air of decisiveness," confided my uncle.

"None of you dared push it?" asked my mother.

"No. After they said that, we had to back down in the face of their suffering and just stay quiet. That's what we decided. All six of us tiptoed out of there without addressing the elephant—or rather, the zombie—in the room!"

"You were the one who should have done it, Féfé," said his wife.

"I think so, too," said my mother. "Who in Jacmel is more qualified than you to talk about zombies?"

"Look, I was on the verge of spilling everything, but I changed my mind at the last moment. For white people, the zombie is just one of those fanciful Haitian ways of dealing with fate. The Siloés would have made a mockery of my memories."

"What memories are you talking about, Uncle Féfé?" I asked.

With an air of great mystery, he pointed directly at me. "Young man, I'm talking about one of life's greatest enigmas!" he announced solemnly. "In our country, it's true: history repeats itself more than it does elsewhere." He put his head in his hands.

"Why all the secrecy?" I asked. "Just tell me, Uncle Féfé."

5

So Spoke My Uncle Féfé

That evening was the first time I ever heard an educated adult, "a man of the law, of substance, and also of the spirits" (as we often laughingly referred to my uncle) take up the zombie question. Up until then, this phenomenon had been more of a mystery to me than the story about getting knocked up by the Holy Ghost's hard-on. As children, zombie stories thrilled us, holding us spellbound and making our hair stand up on end whenever we found ourselves in those storytelling sessions late at night, during long summer vacations in the hills of Jacmel.

According to Uncle Ferdinand, a zombie—man, woman, or child—is a person whose metabolism has been slowed down under the effects of some organic toxin, to the point of giving all appearances of death: general muscular hypotonia, stiffened limbs, imperceptible pulse, absence of breath and ocular reflexes, lowered core temperature, paleness, and failure of the mirror test. But despite these outward signs of death, the zombie actually retains the use of his or her mental faculties. Clinically deceased, interred and buried publicly, he or she is raised from the grave by a witch doctor in the hours following the burial and made to labour in a field (a zombie garden) or in an urban workshop (a zombie factory). Whenever there are doubts as to whether or not someone has died of natural causes, steps are taken to avoid all risk of zombification. It is customary to put a large knife, a razor, or a gun in the hand of the deceased so that they might protect themselves upon being brought back to life. In other cases, the zombie is buried with a ball of thread and an eyeless needle to distract it from the efforts of the zombifiers; or else sesame seeds are put within arm's reach, so as to tempt the unfortunate being to count them one by one during its first night underground. It is not unheard of for people to inject formaldehyde into the veins of a corpse—or a member of the family might ask a pallbearer to break the corpse's bones, to strangle it, or to decapitate it altogether...

6

THE ZOMBIFIER'S SECRET CODE, OR A ZOMBIFEROUS PHARMACOPOEIA

The first stage of the zombification process is the dramatic slowing-down of the metabolism. The *houngan*—the Vodou priest—who creates the zombie arranges things with an accomplice, usually a member of the victim's entourage, who administers the precise dose of a highly toxic substance to the target. The formula for the most well-known zombie poison requires the following ingredients: extracts of dried sea toad, a mule's gallbladder, tibial scrapings from a rabid dog, ground-up bones of a young boy, puffer flesh cartilage, and bones from the middle ear of a garter snake. These ingredients are all ground together in a mortar or using a grindstone, along with a few *tcha-tcha* seeds, some velvet bean sap, a bit of powdered sulphur, and a few mothballs. That mix is then blended into a solution consisting of rum, castor oil, and asafoetida.

Ingesting the drug leads to the apparent cessation of the principle vital functions, which bottom out at about zero, at the point of no return where decomposition otherwise sets in. In the hours following the burial of the zombified body, the witch doctor initiates the reanimation of the bogus cadaver. In order to do this, he gives the victim an antidote composed of zombie-cucumber (devil's trumpet or jimsonweed) and dried leaves from several trees (including cupiuba, pleomele, and guaiacum). These elements are then diluted in a large calabash shell full of seawater that has served previously as the vaginal bath for a woman in her sixth month of pregnancy, or for twin sisters during the half-hour after having sexual intercourse, or two nights before their next menstrual cycle.

Absorbing the antidote is enough to completely reawaken the zombie, in the fullest sense of the term. It keeps the victim from succumbing entirely, releasing the organism from its state of temporary hibernation and allowing it to quickly eliminate the toxins. The cells then move from the weakened state of hypothermia to their normal functions, and the process of oxygenation of the blood, circulating at that point only by fits and starts, returns to its normal rhythm. At this point the subject is ready for the final stage of zombification. The only thing remaining for the witch doctor to do is to remove the individual's *petit bon ange* from its body by manipulating the cosmic forces that connect plants to the spiritual principles of the human condition. Thanks to this exceptional, magical act, the deceased's soul is separated from its body and placed in a bottle.

Uncle Féfé told me about an exploit that had been realized by the witch doctor Okil Okilon, the one who had changed Balthazar Granchiré into an oversexed butterfly. Okilon had inhaled the soul of a rival doctor through a cracked window while the latter was napping one day. He blew it into a crystal carafe. Then, at the cemetery, after a funeral, all he had to do was pass the pitcher's narrow mouth under Dr. Oruno de Niladron's nose to reanimate him. Okilon pulled off a real coup that day.

Most often, the *petit bon ange* thief waits for the false death of his prey to pull the soul he has decided to bottle up out of the living body, using magnetic forces. Thus deprived of its *petit bon ange*, the presumed-dead person is able to speak, to move, to feed itself, and to work. It is limited to a strictly salt-free diet, as salt is known for its anti-demonic properties. The zombie's sense of sight, hearing, smell, taste, and touch, barely altered, function at a slower pace from then on. No longer having a will of its own, the man, woman, or child becomes nothing more than a "come-come," as docile as a mule, totally dependent on the witch doctor, without being, however, what you might otherwise take for a schizophrenic in a state of hysterical catatonia...

7

AFTER TAKING ME through the basic steps of the zombification process, Uncle Féfé reached for a book on one of the shelves in his library.

"Here. Before I go any further, read Article 246 of the Haitian Criminal Code."

I read aloud: "*Also considered attempted murder, by poisoning, is the use of substances that, without causing death, produce a state of lethargy more or less prolonged, no matter how these substances have been deployed and what ensues from their deployment. If, as a result of the state of lethargy induced, the victim is buried, the crime will be considered that of murder.*"

My uncle then brought up two famous cases of zombiism that had once made headlines throughout the country. I had heard Scylla Syllabaire narrate the first story more than once during his evening storytelling sessions in the town square. It was a "classic" of zombie mythology. Told by my uncle, however, it took on a quasi-autobiographical flavour. In effect, Uncle Féfé had personally witnessed the event, on Gonâve Island. It had to do with the same man who had set William Seabrook on the path that led him to publish *The Magic Island* in 1929; this was the serial novel (a best seller in the US) that had made zombies popular in Hollywood during the period between the two World Wars. It was the story of Lil' Joseph, a zombifier. Scylla had told us about him in a tale he called

"The Fugitives of Devil's Hill."

One morning in January 1918, Lil' Joseph and his wife Faith, of the Colombier region, showed up at the HASCO sugar factory leading a party of ragged peasants, all of whom were raring to do some serious cutting on the plantations of the American company. As they were being hired, these men—their expressions dull and their eyes vacant—proved incapable of stating their names. Lil' Joseph had to do it for them. They all came from a small area known as Devil's Hill, an isolated hamlet on the Haitian-Dominican border. It was the first time these workers had ever come down to the plains and been exposed to the noise, the commotion, and the fumes of a modern factory. But Lil' Joseph and his companion assured the foremen that his workers would be exceptionally productive.

Witnesses to the scene realized they were dealing with a zombified workforce—a bunch of poor wretches who had been taken one night from their "final" resting place and made to slave away in the service of a cruel master. Over the course of two weeks, driven by Lil' Joseph's lively whip, they showed themselves to be champion cane-cutters—each cutting three times more than the season's best worker. For twelve straight hours, aside from a brief pause for lunch, it was like they were performing a spectacular ballet—the way they rhythmically advanced from one field to the next, mowing down everything in their path as if hypnotized, under the unforgiving tropical sun. At night, they gathered in their barracks to dig into the abundant food prepared for them by Faith: bland corn porridge, boiled plantains, and black beans seasoned only with garlic and pepper (so as to avoid the vivifying and subversive effects of salt).

Everything was going fine right up until the end of

February. One Sunday, his pockets over owing with cash, Lil' Joseph left for Port-au-Prince to spend some time enjoying the exhilarating parades of the carnival season. He left his team of ragged fieldworkers with Faith, who was perfectly used to watching over them. Early in the afternoon, finding that particular Sunday a little too slow for her liking, Faith had the brilliant idea of bringing her enchanted band of workers for a walk around the neighbouring village of Missions Crossing. Upon arriving, she simply parked her little group in the shade. Adrift outside of time, the zombies had no need to kill it, the way Faith was doing, nibbling (ironically) on various salted candies as she people-watched. All of a sudden, one of the vendors at the market where Faith was strolling about cried out: "Pistachio bars! Ten cents a bag!" They were salted nuts covered in cane sugar. *These are sugar candies, so they'll be the perfect treat for my trusty associates from beyond the grave*, thought Faith. She bought a few bags and distributed them among the zombies. Indeed, they seemed to quite enjoy sucking and chewing on the candies. After just a few moments, however, they all stood up and took off directly for their native Devil's Hill. Once there, they were immediately recognized by their friends and families as the father, brother, fiancé, first cousin, or old friend that had been buried years earlier. Completely indifferent to the confusion they were leaving in their wake, the zombies headed to the tiny rural cemetery where, in the blink of an eye, each dug a new grave and buried himself once and for all...

8

AFTER THE STORY of Lil' Joseph's crew, my uncle moved on to the "Gisèle K. Affair," an incident in which he had been personally involved. He was twenty at the time, and had just begun his advanced studies at Port-au-Prince Law School. Gisèle K., a gorgeous sixteen-year-old girl, came from a family of wealthy exporters, part of the capital's high society. On October 4, 1908, a Sunday afternoon, the young girl suffered an embolism and died on the spot. She was buried the next day with particularly moving pomp and circumstance. But then, eight months later, students from the Sisters of Wisdom School were taking a walk out in the countryside and saw their deceased companion in the courtyard of a remote farm. Dressed in rags, barefoot, but just as beautiful as before her death, she was training a pack of ferocious dogs with the aid of a whip. Upon hearing the news, the girl's parents immediately exhumed the coffin, only to find it entirely filled with coconuts just beginning to rot.

Thanks to the lead provided by the schoolgirls, the police were able to bring the girl back to her home in Verna Woods right away. But her mental state was quite grim. She was sent to Philadelphia, where the eminent American psychiatrists who had taken charge of her care managed to completely restore her health within a year. Once cured, she resolved (with the full support of her loved ones) never to set foot in Haiti again.

In April 1911 (after having played herself alongside Mack Sennett in the very first silent burlesque horror film based on the adventures of a zombie), she left the United States for Paris. The following year, she entered a convent under the name of Sister Lazara of the Christ Child. The last people in Haiti had heard, she had become the Mother Superior of a Carmelite convent in Puy-de-Dôme, not too far from the village of Saint-Gervais-d'Auvergne.

As it turns out, on the Saturday before her false death, my uncle Féfé had expertly deflowered her, after dancing with her until dawn at the ball given by the famous Bellevue Circle Social Club. Their lovemaking in the club's garden had been such a spectacular event that thirty years later, despite the mystical sequel to the drama that had first separated them, every year they exchanged New Year's wishes still ripe with the caresses of that long-ago night.

Uncle Féfé took out a stamped envelope from his pocket. "This is her last letter," he explained. "It's dated December 24, 1937. I received it a week ago. I was planning to read it to Hadriana's parents this morning. You now know why I changed my mind. But here is the most tangible proof of the phenomenon of false death in Haiti. Go ahead and read it..."

Saint-Gervais-d'Auvergne
December 24, 1937

Mr. Ferdinand Paradizot
Jacmel, Haiti

My darling Féfé,
For once I'll take the lead in our traditional exchange
of well wishes. The reason for my impatience is quite
simple: 1938 marks the thirtieth anniversary of my

first *"death."* On October 5, 1908, you were, without a doubt, one of the three or four truly inconsolable people following my casket in that impressive convoy leading to the Port-au-Prince cemetery. I can still recall the intensity of your grief, Féfé. I hear your young voice breaking with passion as you stood over my false corpse.

"I love you, Gise. I'll be grateful all my life for what happened between us last night in the garden of the Bellevue Circle Social Club."

You are often in my prayers. In a few hours, between midnight and the sun rising over the snow, I'll call up the memory of our loving farewell as I listen to the joyful Christmas hymns. On the horizon of our village, that antichrist of Berchtesgaden makes the noise of a hundred thousand devils. His Roman accomplice, for his part, has had the nerve to demand the Holy Father's blessing on the packs of armed young men who've been set loose on our defenceless brethren in Abyssinia.

The news coming from Spain is no better: in hundreds of Spanish villages, nuns are raped in the convents, the militia conduct bloody witches' Sabbaths, interrupting church ceremonies to murder priests and burn down their churches. In all of this, there remains one thing that tortures my poor mulatto soul: for the sake of Catholic Spain, God could have done better than to leave the country in the secular hands of this General Franco and his Moors, *"who fear neither*

God nor man," and are more or less supported by the swastika and that joke of a leader. The Lord's plans are impenetrable. By the blood that runs in my veins, so help me God, that's the truth, Féfé!

Last month, a three-line paragraph in The Cross reported a gruesome massacre of Haitian peasants by one General Léonidas Trujillo in the Dominican Republic. Will you be sure to tell me anything you know about this in your response? This winter, there's a veritable Siberian wind blowing around the stable in Bethlehem. Another reason to keep the spirit of the Divine Child burning in this our (joyful despite it all?) valley of tears.

I'll never forget the year of the final ball of my first life. And so, how is he—my valiant knight of Saturday, October 3, 1908? What a talent you had at twenty years old for "slaying"—through rapture—the romantic, trusting, and, above all, overjoyed young girl I became in your arms, there in the Good Lord's garden!

Always be an upstanding and generous judge, Féfé. May Jesus grant you and your family a happy and healthy 1938. Much love to you.

Your faithful zombie,
Sister Lazara of the Christ Child
(Gise, in your memories)

SECOND MOVEMENT

CHAPTER FIVE

Hadriana-Ache

1

ABOUT THIRTY YEARS after Hadriana Siloé's "evaporation," travellers who ventured out to the town of her birth all came back with the exact same impression: Jacmel had fallen into a state of total decay; Jacmel was nothing but a town adrift. Indeed, everything seemed to prove André Siloé right: the Good Lord had never really taken up residence in our little village. Time, hope, doubt, reason, compassion, tenderness, and even the will to live had all evaporated from Jacmel along with the beauty of his daughter. The place seemed doomed to a dark fate, knocked about by successive trials, and subject, in equally devastating proportion, to those well-known and perpetually unsatisfied troublemakers—desolation and ruin. The Great Fire, hurricanes, droughts, yaws, malaria, the State, erosion, Homo Papadocus—all of these had us caught up in the back-and-forth of some sort of inescapable osmosis. Not one of the witnesses I managed to dig up during my wanderings as a Jacmelian exile had any recollection of the fact that, up until the night of January 29, 1938, the town had been keeping pace more or less harmoniously with the rhythms of a charmed and promising existence, well-attuned to the exuberant free will of each individual.

One afternoon in 1972, in the Latin Quarter, I came upon an article in *Le Monde* that had a different tone than those I had gotten used to seeing over the previous decades. No doubt

RENÉ DEPESTRE

about it, this was the first in at least a quarter of a century
to look beyond those clichéd images of a little city wasting
away from loneliness, and to see the enterprising port—lively,
prosperous, sparkling with civility—that Jacmel had been
at the end of my teenage years, the time of Hadriana Siloé,
during those beautiful and sensual days that came before the
"thin sheet of rainwater evaporating in the heat of the sun."
Here it is, titled "Letter from Jacmel"—that piece I read one
afternoon under the sun-dappled trees of the Luxembourg
Gardens.

2

Letter From Jacmel[1]

Situated in the southern part of the island, on the Caribbean coast, facing Venezuela, Jacmel is the village the farthest away from Port-au-Prince by sea. By land, less than fifty miles separate the two cities. Traveling from one city to the other is the ideal way to discover Haiti—the most beautiful, the most sensual, and the most authentic of all the Caribbean islands. But there is no real road to speak of connecting Port-au-Prince to this little provincial town, once considered the most modern of the island and famous for being, along with the more western town of Jérémie, the village of poets. It is also known for having welcomed, one after the other, two exiled libertadores: Francisco de Miranda and Simón Bolívar. It is even said that Miranda sketched the first Venezuelan flag while docked amongst the coral reefs of Jacmel's windswept harbour. Beyond the fifteen miles recently paved by a French company, there is only a stony dirt and clay road, riddled with potholes, which serves either as path, trail, or water slide, depending on the topography at any given spot. In the dry season it is not too much of a problem, at most three or four hours on foot. But during the rainy season it can take fifteen to twenty hours to cross a hundred or so of the many creeks, often swollen to rapids— if the trip is even manageable at all.

1. Claude Kiejman, "Letter from Jacmel," *Le Monde* (April 1972).

Very few cars ever risk it: a few Jeeps, the odd Volkswagen, and "tap-taps"—one of those half-tank/half-truck vehicles that are Haiti's makeshift form of public transportation—decked out in bright rainbow colours, and sporting equally colourful names: By the Grace of God, Mary the Beautiful, The Renewed Immaculate Conception, Trust in God... Men, women, and children pile up inside, on benches pressed together back-to-front and side-to-side. On the roof, toward the back, and attached to the floor are where you find the animals. Fighting cocks add their war cries to the dizzyingly cacophonous grunting of black pigs of all sizes, tied up, heads bouncing about in the void. "Tap-taps" get stuck many, many times during the trip. When this happens, everyone gets out, rests a bit, stretches, hums a little perhaps. Without any particular urgency, everyone eventually starts pushing and pulling until the vehicle is freed from the muck.

The landscape is intensely tropical. At spots, fierce and untamed, it seems to have been barely touched by man. A confusion of trees, plants, and flowers present the great richness of Haiti's flora: silk-cotton trees, laurel trees, mango trees, sapodillas, tuberoses, orchids, amaranths, oleander bushes, and lilacs. The landscape changes from one hill to the next. Peasants cultivate coffee in their lakous—groupings of wood-frame huts held together with dried mud and lime and packed into tree-branch trellises, in which large extended families live without any basic comforts. Just outside the hut—a pig, a couple of chickens, sometimes a goat, and three stones for a grate to cover the fire. There are a few naked children, with their jet-black eyes, who have never even heard of school. If it is harvest time, the men are in the fields; otherwise they are just there at the entrance to the hut, or lounging in a hammock under the yellow gaze of the dogs.

The women are the heads of the family. They cook, do the laundry, raise the children, and "keep the books." A few times a week, they head to the nearest market, which has been in the same place for generations—at the crossroads of several valleys. They go to sell or barter the things they have grown in their gardens: avocados, mangos, guava, okra, cassava, magic seeds... Wearing simple, light-coloured cotton dresses that stop just above the knee, their hair fixed in dozens of tiny little braids and covered with a scarf knotted at the nape of the neck, each balances an enormous load of merchandise on her head. They go either alone or in groups—their gait elegant, their legs long and taut, always barefoot.

Tireless, silent, pipe in mouth, they walk along single file, discreetly moving to the side in the unusual event of a car passing by. Whenever they need a rest, they crouch down to sit on their heels, legs spread open.

Once the last creek has been crossed, you have arrived in the plain of Jacmel. Already you see the ocean. The land is more fertile. It is a well-known region for growing coffee, which was, it should be noted, along with cotton, the foundation of the island's wealth. In 1895, 25,000 bags of coffee left Jacmel's port headed for Europe; not to mention the cotton, the orange peels for Cointreau production, the goat skins. Back then, Jacmel was an enchanting, flowery, bright, and civilized place—French in its tastes, Creole in its ways, and politically liberal. The town was built facing the sea, and the houses, sculpted of pink wood like those in a Charles Addams drawing, stood side by side next to the shops over owing with goods. Until about 1880, the port in Jacmel was the first and only port on the island regularly serviced by a steamship line.

It was also from Jacmel that travellers from all over Haiti would leave for Europe on the luxurious cruise ships of the Royal Malle line, which could travel to Southampton in just thirteen days, a record for the period. And then also, Jacmel could boast of being one of the rare Haitian towns to have a high school.

Founded in 1864, it still exists today, on its original campus. It was also the first town on the island equipped with a power plant and telephone service.

The Great Fire, coupled with political intrigues, ultimately put an end to this splendour. These days, nostalgia is the problem. The port is sanded up, the great ochre buildings of the customs houses are closed, and all the homes stand shakily in the wake of recent hurricanes, the streets silent and empty. Children play in the gutters, a few women crouch beneath the steps of the iron market, in front of little piles of grains, dried fish, and fruit, waiting for customers. And the pinnacle of refinement: a sign warns in Creole not to soil the boardwalk. There is no longer any telephone service, and the electricity is intermittent, like everywhere in Haiti. On Toussaint Louverture Square, there's the old city hall, where one can still see traces of the words Liberté-Égalité-Fraternité on its façade. Its crumbling walls rise up against the blue of the sky, the ocean peeking through.

On Sunday, with the bells of the six o'clock Mass, and by the grace of God, the town awakens for one day. Led by nuns wearing wimples, hundreds of children in blue-and-white uniforms head toward the church, singing hymns. The market resounds with the noise.

On the roads (or what passes for roads) that lead to the old seaside resort of Raymond-les-Bains, clusters of people in all their finery—women in their pastel-coloured straw boating hats, men in jackets that must have belonged to their grandfathers—seem to have set off on an endless path. In any of Jacmel's three open-air music halls, one can find two or three happy couples enjoying the orchestral rhythms of guitars, marimbas, castanets, or rain sticks.

People still enjoy themselves at the Kraft Sisters' Bed and Breakfast. Run by two elderly women, the little hotel offers weary travellers rooms furnished in an old-fashioned style that include wood-panelled galleries lined by portraits of successive Haitian presidents, including Papa Doc and his son Jean Claude, currently in power. They offer authentic Creole cuisine (sauce à la petite malice, well-seasoned avocados with smoked herring, a stew of roasted chicken rubbed with lemon and spices, potatoes and fried bananas, guava jam, and rum cocktails) served by silent maids who fan you between courses. Jacmel lives in the past with as much intensity as it doubts its own future.

3

HEART POUNDING, I read the first lines of the article, expecting at any moment to find something about the life and false death of Hadriana Siloé. Had the exceptional vitality of her youth not made her, up until the night of her wedding, truly one of the jewels of Jacmel's splendour?

Once I had finished reading, I found myself deeply saddened: not the slightest allusion to Hadriana. The tragic circumstances of her "evaporation" were given no consideration next to the Great Fire, the hurricanes, and the political intrigues that had been identified, and rightly so, as among the plagues that put an end to Jacmel's opulence. The unforgettable beauty of the young French girl had not been acknowledged as one of the causes of the nostalgia that consumed the people of Jacmel. Although it had inspired my departure from my homeland before I had even turned twenty, and had become the cross I bore throughout my years of exile, our collective case of "Hadriana-ache" seemed to have disappeared without leaving any trace in Jacmel's devastated memory.

This was no reflection on the reporter. In all likelihood, she simply had not managed to get any intimate details about the Siloé Affair from her interviewees. Yet the two elderly ladies who ran the Kraft Sisters' Bed and Breakfast were as well suited as I to tell the journalist about the events of 1938.

In fact, they had the considerable advantage over me of having never left Toussaint Louverture Square.

Mélissa and Raissa Kraft had been Hadriana's childhood friends. From kindergarten all the way to their high school graduation, the three had been enrolled together in the Saint Rose of Lima School, located only a few steps away from their respective homes. I had often seen them strolling arm in arm or riding their bikes along the pathways of the town square during those years when the exuberance of their burgeoning womanhood had just begun to beautify the existence of both gods and men. In my eyes, they were the three Creole Graces—already as captivating and inseparable as that trio of Greco-Roman divinities: Aglaea, Thalia, and Euphrosyne. Four years later, on the beach in Raymond-les-Bains, those superbly formed young girls, with their graceful way of strutting about in their swimsuits, barefoot in the sand, were the first to teach me that the female body in motion, all curves and joyful roundness, would soon inspire enormous passion and celebration in my own striking geometrical appendage. Whenever they went by, it would harden—suddenly, unfettered, marvellously!

At Hadriana's wedding, the Kraft sisters stood at the head of a fascinating coterie of bridesmaids, even closer to the action than the luscious Philisbourg twins. Mélissa was the one who had torn her bodice in the church upon seeing her friend collapse. After the "dead" girl's zombification, Mélissa and Raissa, overcome with grief, had imprudently sworn to the patron saints of the parish to abstain from all sexual relations until Hadriana's safe return to the family home. That wait ended up lasting their entire lives. And so, contrary to their natural disposition, their promise compelled them to maintain a cruel celibacy. More than a little aware of their sex appeal, neither one of them found chastity very much to her liking.

4

Imaginary Interview in the Luxembourg Gardens

Holding the "Letter from Jacmel" in my trembling hands, I couldn't help but put myself in the Kraft sisters' place and imagine an interview that would supplement the newspaper story. In my mind, I took the journalist amiably by the arm.

"Come with me, I've got something to share with you about Jacmel's history."

I led the young woman to the balcony on the third floor of the old prefecture. Standing at the iron railing, we had a marvellous view of the entire lower section of the town, by the seafront. It was an exceptionally beautiful twilight. The shadows of the silk-cotton trees on the square faded at our feet. There was no need to protect our eyes from the rays of the setting sun. We could watch comfortably as the light softened into shades of pink and violet on the surface of the sea and on the rusted zinc of the roofs topping the rows and rows of houses, their wood frames darkened by years of bad weather. Pressed up against the fronds of the mango, tamarind, and coconut trees, the houses gave the impression of huddling together fearfully, as if to better resist the stormy proximity of the bay and the seasonal raids of the hurricanes. On the nearby hill that hovered over the pitiful little houses, one could make out a green-and-white colonial-style plantation house surrounded by an extraordinary garden, the wings of the house in perfect harmony with the dwelling's central structure. On the lateral wall running along Orleans Street, four movable shutters pivoted on recessed hinges embedded in the large windows. At the very top of the building, on the sign designating this heavenly place, one could make out a few red letters against a white background: *The Alexandra Manor Hotel*.

"Is it true that the hotel is haunted?" asked C.K.

"Is that what the Kraft sisters told you?"

"No, no. They both remained completely inscrutable when I asked them any questions."

"You should have pressed them. That's the house where one of our schoolmates lived, from her birth until her false death, at nineteen, decked out in her wedding veils."

"Now there's a great beginning for a fairy tale."

"It's something that actually happened in 1938. Feel free to check and double-check the facts. The original name of that hotel was Hadriana Siloé Palace. One month after its grand opening, the proprietor, an American impresario from Cincinnati, Ohio, was compelled by the prefect and the townspeople to replace *Hadriana* with *Alexandra*, the name of his oldest daughter, a very happy wife and mother."

"Would *Hadriana* have brought misfortune to Jacmel?"

"*Hadriana*, written on the façade of the old manor house, would have been a constant knife in the wound that Jacmel had become—an even more atrocious source of anguish than what you described in your article. Too much, just too much for a community that had already had it up to here with history, fire, hurricanes, and political turmoil."

"Was the girl murdered?"

"Worse: allegedly the victim of a heart attack, she disappeared from her grave on the day after her burial! When something like that happens in Haiti, people don't need anyone to paint them a picture. It was clear to us all that a witch doctor had taken the young bride from the cemetery in order to have her serve him. That morning, the news spread like an earthquake."

"Another zombie story! These days, books about your country are full of them. It would seem it comes in cycles. Before leaving Paris, I'd already heard three. Yours is clearly homegrown—in the Kraft sisters' spicy sauce, to boot! Come on, do you really believe in zombies?"

"As recently as last Saturday, a neurologist friend of mine, a pretty dour sort, answered a question just like yours in my presence. *Those who believe in zombies are fools*, he said. *Those who don't are even bigger fools!* That ridiculous dilemma is Haiti's Gordian knot. It's been more than thirty years now that I've been trying, if not to resolve it, then at least to put it out of my mind. But fate, nevertheless, has kept it tucked away in a corner of my handkerchief..."

"To hear you tell it, there's a causal link between the death of this young woman and the decline of your little town. Have I got that right?"

"You've hit the nail on the head. As a result of the events of 1938, even the connection between cause and effect ceased to function normally in Jacmel. The natural affiliation between the real and the supernatural was ruptured by the disappearance of Hadriana Siloé. From then on, all causal links, even the imaginary ones, could have an impact as real as that of Hurricane Inez, one of the most devastating storms ever to hit Jacmel. But let's get back to Hadriana Siloé. Now, where were we?"

"On the early morning of her return to the living."

"Well, it would seem that Hadriana had proven stronger than her kidnappers and, on the day before the zombification ceremony at the cemetery, had managed to give them the slip, thanks in part to the torrential downpour. She'd apparently gone around knocking at several doors, beginning with those of the manor house. But wherever she went, no one answered, and her pursuers were able to recapture her and put her back in captivity."

"The heavy rain must have prevented people from hearing her cries for help, because I don't see French parents turning a deaf ear to the call of their daughter, even if she was coming back to them from the dead!"

"The Siloés slept on the third floor of the manor, in the bedroom farthest away from the ground floor. It's likely that the storm kept them from hearing anything. Everywhere else, people were sleeping not far from their front doors. Look, I don't want to keep anything from you—Hadriana's fists knocked at our door too. My mother, Uncle Ferdinand, his wife, the servants, and, yes, I—the guy who's here talking to you right now—we all woke up with a start. But we stayed curled up under our covers. It was convenient to confuse her desperate pounding with the noise of the driving rain! Like so many other families, caught up in our belief in—and visceral fear of—the power of witch doctors, we were incapable of lifting a finger to save our friend. The Catholics maintained that Jacmel had exposed Hadriana to the worst kinds of risk on the night of her death by deciding, despite the warning of the parish priest and the vicar, to have her wake in the midst of the excesses of a Vodou carnival. But that isn't true; the bacchanalia and all the masks had nothing to do with anything. Christians and heathens, we all gave up Hadriana to her zombifiers for different reasons."

"What do you mean?"

"The effectiveness of magic (I learned this from Lévi-Strauss) is a phenomenon of social consensus. And that's what was working against Hadriana Siloé that night. When an entire village, in accordance with its traditions, is convinced that a human being can become undead as a result of a toxic substance and an act of witchcraft, the victim's entourage can't be expected to come to her aid in such circumstances. On that night back then, in the depths of everyone's conscience, we all just wanted to keep our distance from the young zombie bride, brutally abandoning her to her inescapable fate, seeing her as a danger to the whole of the Jacmelian community. That's what happened."

5

Prolegomena to a Dead-End Essay

All theory is gray, but forever green is the tree of life.
—Goethe

The afternoon of my imaginary interview in the Luxembourg Gardens, as I headed back to my room at the Ségur Hotel, I resolved to let my memory turn back to the events of 1938 and their disastrous consequences on daily life in Jacmel. It wasn't the first time I promised myself—somewhat insistently—to dedicate a book to the subject. My first idea was to talk about Hadriana herself rather than writing an essay on the place and the role of the zombie phenomenon in the deterioration of Jacmel. Is it possible that my homeland was some sort of collective zombie? But after the basic off-the-cuff lesson my uncle Féfé had given me following Hadriana's "evaporation," my inquiries among my friends and neighbours, just like my studies and research abroad, added nothing substantial to my understanding of the zombie's condition. Behind each mystery there were at least a hundred more...

In each text I read on Vodou, there was the obligatory chapter on zombies in Haiti. In every instance, the author seemed somehow to be left short of breath, chasing after an elusive ghost. There was a time when the flood of studies on this element of Haitian sorcery constituted a veritable industry, both within and outside the academic world. It went from the most frenzied sensationalism to the most erudite scholarship. I wanted to offer a personal perspective, situated somewhere between a serialized novel and a monograph—some new and well-thought-out, passionate, and organized tribute to my beloved—that I hoped would raise the debate to a higher plane.

In the early 1960s, I began reflecting seriously on the notes I had gathered. But too often interrupted and ignored over the course of my wanderings, the manuscript never amounted to much of anything. Tossed about from one part of the world to another, I carted it around with me like some pitiful reminder of my failure at Hadriana Siloé's wake.

On the night of April 9, 1972, I unwrapped it for the umpteenth time in twelve years. I fully intended to finish the essay this time around. I began looking over the pages where I had summarized my working hypotheses. I had grouped them into nine propositions under a heading that certainly wasn't appropriate for an essay: "The Jacmelian Adventures of a White *Petit Bon Ange*."

First Proposition
(The Universal Historic Stage)
The zombie phenomenon is situated at the confluence of a variety of mystical trends that have left extraordinary traces at the core of the agrarian sects to which Vodou and its singular "Vodouishness" belong. The rural witch doctor, creator of Haitian zombies— like his homologue from the Middle Ages or the early-baroque era—is a dispenser of good and evil. He is capable of producing either the beneficial charm that

*protects and heals, or the evil charm that persecutes
and destroys.*

Second Proposition
*The nocturnal gangs from the sectes aux yeux rouges
of our (Hadriana and my) Jacmelian childhood have
their roots in either the Italian Frioul archipelago or
in sixteenth-century Lithuania, with the Gascons of
Henri IV, or the traditions of Latin- and German-
speaking Alpine countries. One might also follow the
roots of their magical prowess to societies far removed
from one another in the global sphere, from the
countries of Siberia and Central Asia to the Andean
highlands of South America; from the Pacific islands
to the Nordic territories; from the communities of
Japan, Tibet, and China to sub-Saharan African
societies; from the shores of the Indus River to
Northern Africa.*

Third Proposition
*We have credited witch doctors from all of these diverse
regions of the globe with the capacity to transform
their enemies into animals (werewolf, butterfly,
lizard, crow, rat, ox, cat, lion, leopard, etc.), to engage
in the ritual sacrifice of children, to screw and even
knock up young women remotely, and to take over
the vital substance—spiritual or physical—of other
beings in order to increase their own power in society.*

Fourth Proposition
(The Historic Haitian Stage)
In Haiti, a witch doctor can steal a person's light and

his capacity to dream (his petit bon ange), which he then imprisons—like a ship in a bottle—in an empty bottle of rum, Scott's Emulsion, champagne, or Coca-Cola, as it awaits future magico-genetic operations. During this time, the victim's muscular energy (his gros bon ange) ends up, compelled by a whip, executing the harshest tasks in some part of the countryside. Dissociated beings like these fall, wrists and ankles bound, under the category of human livestock, subject to endless brutality.

Fifth Proposition
The fate of the zombie might be compared to that of the colonial plantation slave of old Saint-Domingue. Its destiny corresponds, on the mystical plane, to that of the Africans deported to the Americas to replace the decimated Indian labour force in the colony's fields, mines, and factories. It would make sense, for the purposes of this study, to determine whether the idea of the zombie is in fact one of the traps of colonial history—something Haitians might have internalized and integrated into their own worldview. It could be a symbol of an imaginary world borne of tobacco, coffee, sugar, cotton, cacao, or spices—one of the many symbols of the ontological shipwreck of man on the American plantations, a perfect fit in the gallery of the wretched of the earth that the writings of Sartre, Memmi, Fanon, and Simone de Beauvoir, among others, have collaged together from various portraits of the colonized (black, Arab, yellow)—not to mention women and Jews.

Sixth Proposition
(On the Process of the Mythological
and Semiotic Vulgarization of Human Reality)
In returning to the original source of the myth, one
must go over with a fine-toothed comb an eminently
magical process that, over the course of the last three
centuries, has allowed for the designating of Europeans
of different ethnicity (Spanish, French, English,
Portuguese, Dutch, Danish, etc.) as "Whites"; of
the indigenous peoples of the Americas "discovered"
by Columbus in the Western hemisphere (Arawaks,
Tainos, Caribs, Ciboneys, Mayas, Incas, Aztecs,
Quechuas, Guaranís, etc.) as "Indians"; and of sub-
Saharan Africans (Sudanese, Guineans, Bantus,
Congolese, Angolans, etc.) as "Negroes," "mixed-race,"
"Mulattos," and "people of colour." Under the effect of
what amounts to an absurdly fantastical inversion of
the hierarchy of form and substance in our species, it
somehow became commonplace to insist on a causal
relationship between the skin colour, facial structure,
and follicular attributes of various human groupings,
on the one hand, and their particular cultural and
natural developments on the other. As a function of
these racialisations of colonial conflicts, the essence
of African ethnicities was reduced to a fantasy of the
"inferior nature of the Negro," while the essence of
the ethnic groups emerging from Europe was elevated
to the no-less-fantastic notion of the "superior nature
of the white man." Through this simultaneously
mythological and semiotic vulgarization, the
institution of slavery invented social types in the

Americas so as to assure its own prosperity. The disguising of souls accompanied the occultation off certain geographical areas: the "West Indies" in the place of the mythical Orient that obsessed Columbus, "America" in the place of Colombia (the admiral's star having dimmed next to that of Amerigo Vespucci). Everything happened as if the enterprising masters of colonization needed, in the magical realm, to put masks both on their field of action and on the protagonists of the triangular crossings that were mobilizing men on three continents (Europe, Africa, and the Americas).

Seventh Proposition
(False Identity)
Haiti, like the other "discovered" lands of the Americas, entered into modern history caught up in this game of masks (white, black, Indian, mulatto, etc.)—that is to say, with a false identity. At the very bottom of the pit that is the reification of men, within the boundaries of death and the separation of the passions, at the tail end of the tragedy of being, is where one encounters the existential time and place of the zombie. Without a personal life or civil status, registered with the local cemetery, torn from the bosom of the family, of the church, of pleasure, dance, sex, friendship, and life itself, bound day and night by the purely physiological and physical exigencies of harsh labour, the zombie adds a fourth episode to the three classic scenarios of black history: brute idiots with backs bent to till the earth; oversized children to be evangelized; angry Black Power militants meant to be rehabilitated

en masse. Within the frame of this ternary destiny governed by the basic barbaric/civilized binary, the zombie represents the ultimate biological fuel—that which remains of Caliban after the loss of his identity, his life having been cut literally in two, his gros bon ange of muscular effort condemned to forced labour in perpetuity and his petit bon ange of knowledge and enlightenment, of innocence and imagination, forever exiled in the first empty bottle within reach.

Eighth Proposition
(Portrait of the Zombie)

These are the elements most critical to fully understanding this sub-Negro—this broken being with neither memory nor vision of the future, with neither needs nor dreams, without roots to bear fruit, without the balls to get a hard-on, this object adrift in the kingdom of shadows, far from the salt and spices of freedom...

It would make sense, at this juncture, to provide an outline of those traits most common to beings trapped in a zombified state: zombies are recognizable by their glassy-eyed gazes, the nasal intonation of their voices, their vacuous expressions, and the fog that envelops their thoughts and words; by their halting manner of walking while looking straight ahead, indifferent to people, animals, things, and plants; by the fact that they instantly degrade everything and anything around them, even without making the slightest bit of contact.

Ninth and Final Proposition
(Zombiehood and Dezombification)
In living its zombified state to the bitter end, might
there be a fresh light of authenticity and freedom
waiting at the end of the tunnel for whatever is left
of that man or woman? Alas, everything would seem
to indicate that there is no possibility for solidarity
in that desert with neither salt nor sympathy that
is zombification. There is no common interest or
passion among zombies. Neither the disdain nor the
hostility of other "races" inspires them to forge any sort
of alliance. Let us join what's left of our animated
bodies together to take action in the name of
freedom! *are words one is unlikely to hear come out*
of a zombie's mouth. Zombiehood has no future. Even
if one were to stuff a bunch of zombies full of sea
salt, they would not find anything better to do than
to hightail it to the nearest cemetery. Once there, just
like Lil' Joseph's crew from Colombier, they would use
their teeth and nails to dig into the rocks and dirt, all
for the supreme satisfaction of liquefying—once settled
back in the earth—into so many stinking carcasses!

Corollary
Why zombies—and zombification—in the Haitian
imagination? Is the myth of the subhuman something
that belongs to the Fourth World of my country? For
whom or for what is the creature a scapegoat? In a
society with a pretty low coefficient of law and liberty,
does the zombie's absolute uncertainty amount to a
mystical manifestation of the extreme desperation of
the human condition that is life on my little half-

island?

That night, reading over all that pseudo-Sartrean jargon mixed up in my vengeful and ludicrous third-worldism, I stopped short, filled with an anxiety that seemed to presage a heart attack.

What about Hadriana Siloé in all of this?

Absent the extraordinary flesh-and-bones zombie who had eluded me for more than thirty years, all I was doing was rambling on about the zombie myth and splitting the finest of metaphysical hairs. There was only one question that really needed to be answered: by what lapse of reason, begetter of monsters and of the living-dead, had the marvellous flesh and the sun filled dream of an adolescent love story been transformed into a shadow wandering across the century?

In the margins of my draft of the essay, I had written in red pencil:

> *Enough with these supposedly keen insights on the mythology and sociology of decolonization. For the second time in this life, Hadriana Siloé is knocking at your door in the middle of the night. Get up and bring your beloved back to her childhood home!*

6

FOUR MORE FRUITLESS years of my life had transpired from the night I gave myself that directive to the moment I managed to go back over every detail of the Siloé Affair. In 1976, I was invited to teach at the University of the West Indies in Kingston, Jamaica. The campus was set on the site of a former colonial plantation that clung to a hill, contained within a luxurious neighbourhood bearing the lovely name Mona. Barely moved into the bungalow I had been assigned to, losing myself in endless contemplation of the island, I experienced a feeling of fullness and well-being matched only by the wonderment I had felt in those long-ago days when Hadriana was alive. For the first time since leaving Jacmel, I was able to think without sadness about all those years of failure and guilt that stretched behind me in the swirling *elsewhere* of Haiti and had taken me on a frantic quest for the young girl. I finally stopped living her memory as an experience of mourning and nostalgia. I was no longer personally tortured or wounded by the misfortunes of my homeland or by the overall lack of goodness in the world.

As I wandered around campus or up and down the sunny, laughing hills of Kingston, I no longer felt compelled to tell myself every fifteen minutes: *If you turn to the right, after fifty yards, you'll run into Hadriana Siloé*, as I had done so many times in streets around the world, from Rio to Paris, from

Prague to Hanoi, from Tangier to Dar es Salaam, from New York to Kyoto, from Havana to Valparaíso. I had been given the opportunity to teach a course called "The Aesthetics of American Magical Realism" to a group of young people—they were over owing with imagination and humour, glistening with jovial and liberated intelligence, with probity and intellectual creativity, and free from any remote-controlled pantomime directed by some state force operating in their individual consciences.

In earlier days, under less hospitable skies, I had found myself stuck in a sort of "zombie cocoon," surrounded by false colleagues and friends, given a false university chair, looking into the "preprogrammed" eyes of false students. My classes back then had left me broken, exasperated, short of breath, my mind and body bled dry by an all-encompassing socialism.

In Mona, silos of joy and hopefulness rose up within me. The beautiful students—black, blond, and everything in between—drank up my words while letting their rosy tongues roam sensuously across their moist lips. They crossed their legs high on the thigh, exposing themselves to the yearnings of my frustrated single man's lust with their fleshy curves ready for the most delightful ploughing. At the end of the class, laughing and tittering merrily, a swarm of warm and tender young girls would cluster around my podium, closing in insistently with their sweet feminine embrace, offering all sorts of brilliant observations on the role of the marvellous and the beautiful in the formation of Caribbean culture. These courses helped me rid myself of the old adolescent anguish that clung to my skin, and to integrate the painful memories of Jacmel into my adult self. With each class, I felt as if I had regained fresh vitality for renewed creation. I would go back to my bungalow energized enough to go jogging, to play some tennis, or to go swimming, buoyed by a feeling of sated physical love and glorious victory over loneliness.

Early one morning, sitting down to my desk, I noticed with relief that I was finally ready—that is, without the usual feeling of distress, and using the French language—to make my peace with the natural, the comical, the playful, the sensual, and the magical aspects of Jacmel's painful past. I, who until then had not written anything but ridiculous pastiches of other people's poetry—I was able to write, in a single breath, a long poem, of which one stanza ended up perfectly foretelling what was to happen just a few months later:

> *Once, many years*
> *before the death of my body,*
> *I was dead in spirit,*
> *laid out stone-dead,*
> *my dreams adrift*
> *like a bridal veil*
> *spiralling in the wind,*
> *all my senses were dulled,*
> *suddenly one of our islands brought me back*
> *to the madness of a woman,*
> *to the time of Hadrina Siloé,*
> *the mirror that takes root*
> *in an almond-shaped sun.*

On that morning, with the great looking glass of poetry in hand, I took a different path in my thinking about Jacmel. The *flammentod* (stirrings) of a rediscovered adolescence set a fire in my memory, producing the chapters of this chronicle. I wrote the first thirty pages in a single stroke. At last I had the key with which to make sense of the dramatic events of

1938. But in those days of intense creation, I never for a single second considered the possibility that my voyage through the world of words would put me on the real path to finding the false-dead woman who, after a thousand detours throughout the world, had been harnessed to my existence for the past forty years. On Wednesday, May 11, 1977, at six in the evening, at the University of the West Indies in Mona, I was finishing up my aesthetics class when Hadriana Siloé entered silently into the amphitheatre through one of the doors in the back. I immediately recognized her gray-green eyes—sharp, almond-shaped, with the same beaming, sun filled gaze I remembered. The oval of her face, the fruit of her mouth, the honey of her hair, the brightness of her flesh had ripened with age—in the prime of her life, she possessed charms as irresistible as those that had enthralled me as a youth. What I felt on seeing Hadriana in my classroom simply cannot be compared to anything else that has ever happened to me. I was trembling from head to toe in a state of near-religious rapture, immersed in the sensory drunkenness of my whole being, lips and imagination suddenly aflame, a raging charge infusing my remarks on the techniques by which Caribbean writers perceived and expressed the supernatural of everyday life in their literature. My students were amazed and thought for a moment that I had entered a transcendental state, all to show them the true qualities of the supernatural and the beautiful within our literature.

"I hope very soon to be able to convince you," I exclaimed, exalted, trembling, "that there exists, perhaps at this cultural crossroads more than anywhere else, a 'metaphysics of beings and places' that obeys the strange logic of dreams! The other evening, when I told you about the story I'd finished the night before, I said that its oneiric epicentre was a manor house where there lived a woman who, *more beautiful than the very world we inhabit*, had never ceased to embody, in my eyes, the secrets of eternal beauty. I told you the story of Hadriana Siloé, but wasn't able to give you any recent news about her life or her death. You shared in my impossible hope to someday hear her unravel, in her own words, the mystery of her 'evaporation' on January 31, 1938. Hosanna! Our dream has come true. Hadriana Siloé is among us! Her beauty shines at the back of this very room!"

The class joined me in a round of thunderous applause. A number of young men and women carried her, triumphant, up to my podium, which she bathed in her radiance. We all had tears in our eyes. We decided on the spot to have a party in her honour. She opened her home to us, in the hills of Kingston, up in the Blue Mountains. It became a veritable game among my students to phone their many friends and to try to find a band ready to enliven the party with the songs of Bob Marley. We headed off separately in an explosion of joy after making plans to reunite at Hadriana's home at nine o'clock.

Once the students had left, we found ourselves alone together, face-to-face, she and I, caught up in the wonder of our reunion. Without speaking a word, we left the classroom hand in hand. A harmonious backdrop of seagulls and stars welcomed us into the warm night. We walked in silence along the well-lit lanes leading to my bungalow. We had too much to say to one another. We did not know where to begin. Bursts of love passed through me like the piercing flash of headlights. Fear of ridicule stirred in my guts with a terrible force. The campus's stately, tropical trees passed by in a blur, like rays from the wheel of destiny that guided our stumbling steps. I dove in, eyes closed:

You came and thus did the fire rekindle itself
The shadow yielded, the cold below frosted
And the earth covered itself with your fair flesh.[2]

"Patrick, I pray I haven't misunderstood."

"Hope has arisen from the smoke..."

"*... and the dust,*" she said. "Please don't let this be a dream."

Our hands stopped trembling. We turned to one another, opening the floodgates of the years to the waves of our caresses. To this day, Hadriana and I are incapable of explaining how we managed to cover those hundred yards of grass leading up to the bungalow. Perhaps our kisses, passionate and ravenous, created some sort of protective railing along the steep slope that led to my bed. From the first moment it was good—dizzying, delicious, wild.

Following the unforgettable celebration organized for us by Kingston's youth, the sun rose to the sound of our orgasms on Thursday, May 12, 1977—a day as blue as the mountains that have sheltered our passion ever since. When we awoke later that afternoon in Hadriana's home, I let her read my tale of her extraordinary past. She then opened her desk drawer and handed me the chronicle of her zombie adventure, exactly as she had lived it from Saturday the twenty-ninth to Monday the thirty first of January, 1938.

---

2. Paul Éluard, "Death Loves Life," in *The Phoenix* (Éditions Seghers, 1954).

THIRD MOVEMENT

CHAPTER SIX

HADRIANA'S TALE

You depart to that deep place of the dead, neither struck by wasting sickness, nor having won the wages of the sword...
—Sophocles, Antigone

1

I DIED ON the night of the most beautiful day of my life: I died on the night of my marriage in the Saint Philippe and Saint Jacques Church. Everyone thought I had been struck down by the sacramental Yes that burst out of me. It was said that I had been swept away by the fire of my consent, overcome by the depth of its power and truth—that I had been done in by my own bridal passion.

Truth be told, my false death had begun half an hour before I cried out in the church. Before the bridal party departed to head to the church, I was already completely ready to leave. I took a final look at myself in the sitting room mirror. *Let's go, Hadriana!* said a voice inside me. It was excessively hot, and at the base of the stairs, amidst the affectionate chattering of my bridesmaids, I mentioned how thirsty I was.

"I'd love a glass of ice water."

Mélissa Kraft immediately volunteered to go get me one, but I did not give her the chance. In my full bridal regalia, I charged toward the pantry—speeding through the manor as I had always done. I was faster than my friends. Had someone anticipated my last-minute thirst? A pitcher of lemonade awaited me on the oak dresser, plain as day. I poured myself a tumbler-full, then a second, then a third, drinking each glass to the very last drop until my thirst was entirely quenched. In the heat of that nuptial oven, the cool lemonade was intoxicating. For days, making the most banal gestures had felt as exhilarating as the wedding itself. The emotions of every moment thrilled me.

As I emerged onto Orleans Street, a joyful din arose from the town square.

"Long live the bride! Long live Nana!"

It was truly that general state of jubilation that people in Jacmel had been talking about for the past several days: confetti, garlands, and orange blossoms rained down on my path, mixed with hand-clapping and shouts of adulation. Young girls were crying tears of joy! Some part of me also felt like crying. But laughter blocked its path through my eyes, my mouth, the rapture of my skin... I moved forward—sunlit, ecstatic on the gallant arm of my devoted father. On Church Street, on the Sorels' balcony, a little boy cried out: "Here's a kiss for you, Nana!"

I wanted to send one right back to him. But it was too late: I was dying. Just a moment prior, a terrifying unease had started to come over me. A sharp tingling had begun coursing through me, as if I were being pricked with needles from head to toe. I couldn't breathe. I was suffocating under my veil. My father, though right by my side, noticed nothing. Standing proudly in his tuxedo, he helped me respond to the cheering crowd. No one noticed the state that I was in. On the square just in front of the church, I saw my fiancé Hector on the arm of Mam Diani, my friend Patrick's mother. And Hector saw me for the first time in my bridal gown; the idea that he would soon be able to take it off me was completely blinding him. He could not see that the hands of death had been the first to slip under my dress, rustling with dreams.

2

WITH MY FIRST steps inside the church, I thought my legs would give out before I could make it to the altar. The sounds, the colours, the lights, the smells—they made a jumble of confused impressions on my muddled senses. I could not make out the difference between the sound of the organ and the flicker of a candle, between my own name and the green banners, between the smell of the incense and the bitter flavour that was burning my taste buds. I moved forward, groping as I went, through a sort of effervescent tar. I found myself kneeling in front of a wide well: I pulled myself together and concentrated what life I had left on my sense of hearing. I felt as if I were swimming desperately in viscous, bituminous water toward the most fantastic object in the world: my fiancé, Hector Danoze, just to my right, his flesh turned shapeless and phosphorescent. He had become nothing more than three giant letters that spelled out *YES*. My frantic swimming sought only to reach that goal as it first came close, then moved away, liquefied into a stream of lava that enveloped Hector, the priests, the altar, the hymns, the decorations, the attendees, the sky beyond the apse. This empyreumatic sound light-body, on one of its backward surges, suddenly threw itself at me. It lodged itself in my genitals. And my genitals came together as a final sigh that began climbing up through my body like the rising mercury of a barometer. I felt its upward movement in my guts, then in my digestive tract. It left a strange emptiness in its wake. It stopped for a few moments at my heart, which was barely beating. Was the sigh of my sex going to take its place? I felt it rise up through my throat. It nearly choked me before finally settling its burning weight on my tongue. With the four lips of my true mouth, I screamed the ultimate Yes of life to my Hector and to the world!

"Hadriana Siloé is dead!" the voice of Dr. Sorapal rang out above my lifeless body.

I heard a tumult of overturned chairs and benches, a racket in Creole, a clamouring whirlwind of panic. In the midst of all this, I could make out Lolita Philisbourg's sensual, dramatic soprano. It seemed as if people were ripping fabric all over the church. Something fell down just next to me, and then someone cried out: "Hector is dead too!"

It seemed he had followed me to the grave. The voice of Father Naélo snapped me out of this first dream within my dream: "Hadriana Siloé has been taken from us at the moment of her marriage. The scandal has occurred in the house of the Father!"

Someone's arms lifted me off the church floor. Whose could they be? I would have recognized immediately those of my father, Hector, or Patrick. The man had trouble pushing through the crowd of attendees. My dangling feet knocked into people as we passed. A hand grabbed my right foot. It held on for a long time. I felt the cool evening air despite the death mask that had been welded onto my face. The bells chimed with their full force, the backdrop to the cheers and hand-clapping, just as before. Whoever was holding me began to run. Several others ran alongside us noisily. Of all my senses, only my hearing still functioned. A woman's voice cried out: "Long live the happy couple!"

Immediately, the carnival began on the town square. I noticed that I could smile—laugh, even—from within my misfortune. I had my first giggling fit of the night—people were doing carnival dances all around me; drums and *vaksin* were going wild. I felt as if the man carrying me was also dancing. My stiffened limbs were incapable of joining him. As soon as whoever it was had crossed the manor's doorstep, my sense of smell immediately came back to me: it was the smell of the waxed floor of my childhood. The man placed me carefully on one of the sitting room rugs.

3

THERE WAS A furious commotion all around me, punctuated intermittently by sobs and exclamations. I could hear the sadness and surprise in my girlfriends' bitter utterances— admiration and anger in those of my male friends. At one point, I felt someone leaning over me. A hand took hold of my wrist; another moved what must have been a stethoscope to different spots on my chest. The people attached to these hands exchanged a few words. From their voices, I understood they were Dr. Sorapal and Dr. Braget. Once again, I wanted to laugh. Young Dr. Braget, ever since his return from Paris, would say to me every time we met: "When are the Siloés going to switch family doctors? I'd so love to watch over the health of their daughter." And now, his hand in my blouse, he was feeling my breasts. Would he realize that they were still full of life? My optimism did not last long.

He placed something on my mouth. "Negative," he murmured to his older colleague.

"She has no pulse," said Dr. Sorapal.

"Her breasts are still warm. Splendid, fresh fruits! It's like they're still alive!"

"A dying star continues to shine, my friend! Check her eyes."

Dr. Braget parted my eyelids. I saw him, but the fervent gaze in his catlike brown eyes, misty with tears, could not see me back!

"No ocular reflex," he said.

"All that remains is to prepare the burial license. It's official: stiff limbs, no respiratory or ocular reflex, no pulse, diminishing core temperature. Heart attack."

"Son of a bitch!" exclaimed Dr. Braget.

"Damned myocardial infarction!"

They cursed death instead of deepening their exam. I focused on my sense of sight: perhaps there would be a glimmer, the flicker of an eyelid. As he ran his fingers through my hair, Dr. Braget's face was suffused with tears.

Dr. Sorapal kept chewing on his lower lip. "The saddest night of my long life," he said.

"It's my Waterloo," said the other one, the Don Juan.

4

THE CORNER OF the sitting room where I had been laid out was dimly lit. Mama had come over to cover my body with a sheet. When it was time to cover my face, she changed her mind. In tears, she caressed my face. My father joined her; he kneeled down by my side. I felt sorry for them—for all three of us. I wanted to cry, but could not. My parents had to be brought away, and Patrick took their place. He clasped my hands in his, and he looked deep into my eyes. He kept calling out my nickname with an infinite tenderness. He, too, went away sobbing.

Everything in the sitting room had been moved. The mirror, covered in flour and hanging just above me, looked like some sort of Pierrot, hilarious in its white mask. From the other end of the room came Madame Losange's voice (polygonal, with rounded angles and far more than three sides, as Hector had always said). She had strongly suggested to my girlfriends that they turn their underwear inside out. The Philisbourg twins, Mélissa Kraft, and Olga Ximilien were the first to comply. Then she said to all present that my death was unnatural. She told the story of Balthazar Granchiré, the butterfly. I was brought back to a story from long ago, similar to the ones my old servant Felicia used to tell me before bed when I was a little girl. And now it was the story of my final repose. Klariklé Philisbourg had told me about a diabolic *deflowering* butterfly. Apparently, my godmother had taken the creature as her lover in the months leading up to her death. I was meant to be next. We had had a good laugh at that idea, Hector and I. Not for nothing, Jacmel had always been known as a magical place. After that, the question arose as to where to display my body for the wake. Patrick's uncle, good old Uncle Féfé, proposed Lovers Lane! Maître Homaire declared that I belonged to the realm of the stars. He added something about the birds. A moment later, Madame Losange went back on the attack: she said something about needing to deflower me. I knew from Felicia that this was common in the countryside whenever it was deemed possible that a sorcerer had "bottled up the *petit bon ange* of a young virgin."

There was some sort of debate about who should be the one to do it. Madame Losange vetoed Lolita, given that she was a twin. Someone else said that the job should be done by a fellow innocent. "Why not Patrick Altamont?" they said. My dear Patrick—I would have loved to see that!

Mam Diani flew to his rescue: "Nana and my son were held by the same woman over the same baptismal font. They're like brother and sister."

Actually, Patrick very well could have been the one to open me up. It was the summer before I met Hector. At a holiday resort in nearby Meyer one night, we had wandered away from the others down a path that led to the beach. I was his for the taking. Would he be the one to penetrate me? His hand trembled between my legs. We had run down the hill in the light of a gentle moon that loomed over the empty sea. He had complete liberty to plunge into the mysterious waters of my flesh. He caressed me gently, with the amazement of a teenager who could not believe his clumsy hand was actually lying there, starstruck, on the mound of my ripe almond! He had something pretty impressive going on himself: not your average little dickie or some sweet diddly wee-wee—more like a magnificent piece of manhood, ready for a spectacular nocturnal voyage. But we contented ourselves with gazing quietly over the Caribbean Sea!

5

I saw two men in black cassocks bend over me before heading toward the well-lit part of the sitting room: it was Father Naélo and Father Maxitel. Once they arrived, several others, who had been scattered about up until then, moved their chairs closer to the sofa where my parents were seated. Then there was a long discussion in hushed tones. They were making plans for my wake and burial. The house was abuzz with all sorts of sounds: steps on the staircase, an incessant coming and going on the ground and first floors. The sounds of the carnival were muffled, as the windows that opened out onto Orleans Street were closed. In the sitting room, the whispering seemed to go on and on. No one else came to see me. Bored to death, as it were, I had fallen into a deep sleep inside of my final sleep. In it, I had the following dream: I was a powerful kite—red, white, and blue, like the colours of my homeland. I had a long, knotted tail: a strip of cloth fitted with razor blades and glass shards. I looked just like one of those multicoloured kites from the heated competitions young Jacmelians often play on the beach. In the 1930s, upon returning from High Mass every Sunday, the spectacle of colourful kites used to greet me in the skies above our balcony—just over half a mile away, as the crow flies. Some days, more than fifty little boys and grown men, facing into the wind of the bay, tugged fearlessly on their kites made of paper or light fabric. In my dream, my skin was stretched across a bamboo frame, and there were only four of us kites on this morning—our colours battling for space a few hundred feet above the magnificent waves. Hector, my pilot on the ground, held tight to my string: he would set me off on an abrupt descent, only to help me climb even higher, with slight feints to the right and left so as to catch the strings of my adversaries by surprise with the razors and sharp glass affixed to my tail. The flight, in the heat of the sun, had me downright tipsy! I was getting drunk—an eagle, feathers blowing in the wind, talons unsheathed, I charged at the nearest prey. It didn't take long for me to knock out two of the most formidable enemy kites. There was still one huge blue-and-red kite remaining. In my dream, I figured out that it was an aerial tournament between France and Haiti: red, white, and blue versus red and blue. What would my fiancé—the Haitian controlling my every movement—decide to do? My dream threatened to become a nightmare as I turned from a kite into a small plane. I suddenly found myself on the balcony of the manor, whereas Hector was still holding the joystick of the single-seater aircraft. I was waving a handkerchief, sending him kisses. Before disappearing into the distance, he spelled out my name in pink smoke in the azure of the bay. I woke up to this vision of happiness.

I had first met Hector in very similar circumstances: one Saturday morning, two days after receiving his pilot's license in Port-au-Prince (he was one of the first three pilots trained in the country by American aviators), he had arrived from the direction of the sea, like an arrow pointed at the manor house, a veritable conqueror of the skies. Attracted by the humming of his little plane, I had rushed out to the balcony to see the words, *HADRIANA, I LOVE YOU!* above me. After landing, he called me from the capital. We spoke on the phone for two hours—and for another two the next day, and each day after that, until his return to Jacmel the following weekend. We did not leave one another's side for the next forty-eight hours—stampeding down to Raymond-les-Bains Beach first thing in the morning for a wild sunrise swim, tennis in the afternoon, dancing at night, followed by a stroll along the beach leading up to an exquisite midnight stopover in the garden. From the very first night he, too, could have opened me right up—to the point where I had come to think of my virgin's ripe almond as Hector's very own box of dreams. But he dreamed of an act of love blessed in a church, by Father Naélo. And now he was in the hospital in a state of shock, with me walled up in my false death. Fate was punishing me for a sin I had not even committed. Hadriana knocked out, down for more than ten seconds on the church floor at her own wedding, disqualified from the spectacular combat of her honeymoon, from the work-of-the-flesh-only-aftermarriage, as Hector had wanted it. Ashamed of his apostolic aviator's erection, he had placed a hand over it, scared stiff by the possibility of committing a mortal sin. He was afraid to dirty the white skin of the French fairy, Creole daughter of a prince of mathematics and tobacco. I spent my honeymoon—my tar-moon, really—on a parquet floor that smelled of childhood and zombies, a few hours before my burial and my consecration as one of the living-dead. A terrific wave of distress enveloped me and I tumbled into it headfirst before losing consciousness.

6

When I finally came to, I found myself on the town square, stretched out between the candles dotting Lovers Lane. Strangely, I felt as if I myself was leaning out the window, observing what all the masked people were doing there, standing around a catafalque underneath the silk-cotton trees rattling with the sound of terrified birds. I disappeared from the window frame of the third floor only to reappear, naked, on the floor below. Every so often, over the course of the night, I let myself go in this doubling game that was taking me from childhood to death, from the little girl riding her bicycle around the town square to the teenager strolling along with the Kraft sisters. My fainting spell had made me miss my chance during the preparation of my body: I had hoped that upon touching my flesh, the person who had been tasked with arranging my body for its horrible fate would end up discovering the truth of my false death. I was still wearing my bridal gown—veils and all. Indeed, I had gone through with the marriage sacrament by pronouncing that formidable, famished *Yes*. My perception had improved since the knockout at the church. I could hear just about everything. From time to time I could even see a bit—my sight coming and going. I felt the cool softness of the filmy fabric. The crown of orange blossoms was still on my head; the twinkling stellar cupola of the night sky within my reach. The vast space sparkling with stars seemed to want to become part of my body. The moon came back in full force and settled in my fertile ovaries. All I would have had to do was stretch out my hand and bring one of the stars to my lap, to take the place of my empty ripe almond—stuck there in the midst of one of the most wonderfully starry nights of our lives. But my hands could not bring anything close to me. Nailed to the cross of my false death, crucified on a dream buried within a dream, I could only hear the silence of the carnival to my left as it deepened a lesser mystery at the centre of the great mystery of what was happening to my destiny. Again there was some debate about me. I was an apple of discord among the living. Cécilia Ramonet wanted to protect the wake from the excesses of the Vodou gods. Maître Homaire made a point regarding my great love for life. "And now her beautiful legs are trapped in that padded box." One thing he said was very true: even in my coffin I was far closer to a carnival drum than to the tolling of church bells. Father Maxitel reprimanded Maître Homaire, accusing him of profaning a saint. Me—a saint? You know, I managed—not once, but twice, Father— to offer my body, eyes closed, to another being, well before the lifting of the "not-until-marriage" bond: Patrick was but a single blond hair away from getting over the paralysing fact of his awkward adolescent hand on my ripe almond and taking a proper manly dip into the passionately consenting waters of my womanhood. With Hector, from the very first night, it was the same scenario: my box of dreams had been ready and willing to reveal the last of its virgin secrets. A saint— really? Reverend Father, excuse me, but I have sinned! Another time, one overheated August afternoon, with the door to the balcony flung wide open against the sky above the bay, I was nude in my bedroom with Lolita Philisbourg. The black-and-purple coal of my seventeen-year-old sex cried out in the burning embers of her caresses. I was electrified by her mouth on my peach, riper than any other fruit in season, be it Haitian mango or French melon. It was incredible, Father, hearing the song of the birds outside as Lolita cultivated my springtime garden. It was wonderful, delivering my inflamed Creole flower, my untamed love box, to my best friend's tongue, as she brought me dizzyingly to seventh heaven with three, five, up to seven orgasms in a row on that blessed day. Dr. Braget argued that the *banda* should be seen as a form of prayer. A *banda* dancer himself, it was surprising that he had not been able to distinguish my living breasts from a pair of tits ready for the morgue. Dear Henrik Radsen, Papa's best friend, had gone even further: he lauded every dance of the pelvis and buttocks as the oratory form that gave Haiti all its charm in the eyes of the white Western God. General César spoke of the second death that awaited me, prey to the bestial rutting of Baron-Samedi. And what if the Haitian gods chose their lovers from among zombies? What if a certain sex-maniac, fully-loaded-machine-gun of a butterfly was already setting up at the cemetery, waiting for his chance to launch an attack on the Siloés' Maginot Line? My ear caught the words of the ever-faithful Mam Diani: she had seen me "transform from a little tyke into an exceptional beauty." She remembered what I had once told her in confidence: if ever I should die young, instead of prayers and tears at my wake, I wanted a carnival of five hundred devils!

I got my devils after all—my wake was hit by the lightning bolt of their five hundred "Magic Balls"!

7

I MUST HAVE dropped off again, as I was abruptly awakened by a bugle call, a tremendous reveille on the other end of the square, soon drowned out by the *rada* drums. I could not see people dancing, but from the cadence of their steps I was able to picture the movement of their knees, hips, and shoulders. There was a drum break: in homage to my death the crowd went into a *cadavre-collectif*. Then a soldier approached my catafalque. He shined a flashlight on my face. It was Captain Armantus. He seemed to be listening to me like I was telling him something very serious. His face suddenly took on a terrified expression, as if he had seen some horrible monster in my place. His eyes bulged out of his head, and he could not finish his military salute. He screamed like a hunted animal. I shuddered so intensely I thought my blood, which was then circulating in fits and starts, was going to resume its natural rhythm. I once again heard the bugle call for the dead.

Indeed, I had fallen on the battlefield. After the captain's precipitous exit, there was a strange void all around me, a deathly silence. All my ears could pick up was the gentle flickering of the burning candles. Suddenly, the piercing cries of a sow being sacrificed! Too much, it was too much: I was seized with violent internal spasms. All my bones vibrated to the point of breaking. I sank into a nightmare buried inside my nightmare. I was being robbed of my essence. My *petit bon ange* was being separated from my *gros bon ange*. The former was being put into a calabash to be brought on the back of a mule to a penitentiary for souls on a mountain in Haut-Cap-Rouge. The latter, arms tied behind its back, was being prodded in the opposite direction with lashes of a whip. All ties had been broken between the two parts of my being. After hours of climbing, the mule carrying my *petit bon ange* passed through a heavy wooden gate. An old black man, in passably good shape, received me smilingly.

"Madame Danoze, I welcome you to the prison of thoughts and dreams. This inner house, where, for a variety of reasons, the souls of thousands of *petit bon anges* are peacefully spending the rest of their days, will be your home from now on. This detention centre has been equipped to hold the contained souls of good people condemned to lose their spiritual freedom. The cellular process consists of bottling up the imagination of individuals transformed into the living-dead. The bottles you'll see are a whole host of dungeons made of glass, crystal, metal, porcelain, leather, earth, and stone!"

My amiable jailer brought me into a subterranean gallery brightly illuminated by dozens of lamps. The four walls were covered from floor to ceiling with crates full of bottles. It was a veritable museum of bottles: round, square, flat, tubular, wicker, potbellied, large-bottomed—they ranged from vials to carboys, from flagons to decanters, from oil to vinegar cruets, from small jugs to wine bottles, from carafes to measuring glasses, from flasks to demijohns, from mini–champagne bottles to siphons, from magnums to jeroboams!

"Each of these containers," said the guard, "bears a label where the former identity of the bottled soul is written. Don't be afraid to come closer, madame, the beings we keep here are as harmless as butterflies. Here, let me tell you about a few of your cellmates—I'll choose at random. In this old jar of Vicks VapoRub we have a babbling *petit bon ange* taken straight from the cradle, a Syrian merchant's child. There's a commodities trader meditating in this pitcher over here. The occupant of this bohemian crystal carafe is a Marine Corps sergeant. This milk jug contains a little shoemaker's *petit bon ange*. This demijohn over here holds the soul of Brother Jules, a Breton schoolteacher. Right next to it is the soul of an ex-president of the republic. A little farther away, in that liquor bottle, a Surrealist poet is busy contemplating something or other. And in this alchemist's beaker presides an Anglican bishop. There's a homosexual painter incarcerated in that bottle of seltzer water, and a colonel from the Haitian National Guard in that wicker stein. And finally, we have here the *petit bon ange* of a Mater Dolorosa right next to that of a Little Poucet. As for you, madame, given both your beauty and your nobility, you'll be sealed in this old jeroboam of champagne. It was once kept in the cellar of a Norwegian king from the baroque era. Your label has already been prepared: *Petit bon ange of a French femme-jardin*. In the absence of sweet dreams (since *petit bon anges* don't dream), you will be free, like a canary in a cage, to trill to your own song, without any longing for your *gros bon ange*, which now serves the desires of a famous Baron-Samedi in the mountains of the northeast!"

Immediately thrust into the royal bottle, my *petit bon ange* awakened in the false cadaver displayed on the central square in the midst of a raging carnival...

8

I THEN SAW Madame Losange in a red blouse and a grenadier's tricornered hat. She was not the only one bustling around the chapel. She was dancing—which dance was it again? Maybe a *yanvalou-dos-bas?*—with a young girl in a wedding veil. I could only see their upper torsos as they bent forward and straightened up, like small boats racing on a furious sea. I saw the stranger, a very beautiful black girl, remove her veil and move toward my coffin. She was completely naked. She bent over me and let her breasts hang above me. I wanted to bite into their vivacious feast: huge breasts swollen with life and lyricism, round, firm, suspended above my famished abyss. I recognized my own breasts disguised in the bosom of this black girl participating in my marriage carnival. She then used her veil as a bath towel and wiped death's funereal dew off her body. At that moment, the rhythm of the drums changed suddenly into a *nago-grand-coup*, to bring the wake to its climax. I was surrounded by masked revellers swept up in the diabolic communal farandole. History itself seemed to be parading around the catafalque. I could identify various historical figures mixed in with the traditional costumes of a Jacmelian carnival. There were masks of marquises and pirates from long ago. Old regime soldiers accompanied by Marines and Benedictine monks appeared in my honour. Thanks to the images I had seen in schoolbooks, I easily recognized Toussaint

Louverture, Simón Bolívar, King Christophe, Dessalines, and a stocky, moustached white man—a contemporary figure I had seen in the journal *L'Illustration*: it was Stalin himself, wearing the elegant garb of a czar. His mischievous little eyes stayed fixed on me as he held on tightly to the woman of his dreams, Pauline Bonaparte, fascinating in her whiteness. Noticing him so thrilled to see me, a desperate hope popped into my head: maybe I was also part of the carnival, playing the role of Sleeping Beauty—my seeming death and everything that had happened since the beginning of the evening merely episodes from the famously prolonged sleep in that fairy tale. By dawn, I would once again be Hadriana Siloé, just as Pauline Bonaparte would return to her young dressmaker's body, Bolívar to his frail shoemaker or tailor's shoulders, Sir Francis Drake to his familiar dockworker's gait, Joseph Stalin to his short-legged provincial notary's stance and talent at playing the harmonica. I would finally become the prized spouse of the aviator Hector Danoze, well on my way to the at-long-last-sanctioned festivities of my honeymoon.

A gunshot snapped me out of this last dream nestled within my dream. A moment later, someone cried out: "Down with Granchiré! Nana is resurrected!"

Nothing had changed as far as my living-death was concerned. The birds made their startled presence known in the silk-cotton trees. I must have been enormously intriguing to them, flanked by candles in the blue of the day. Madame Losange, still wearing her imperial grenadier's outfit, traced the sign of the cross on my forehead with hot ashes. Her partner in this dream, before blessing me, showed me once more those breasts that were twins of my own under the transparent veil. I then heard the stark chiming of the bells of Jacmel: after the mad, rushing eighth notes of the night before, sombre white and black notes rained down on my desert, one by one, like so many drops of metal, in the place of the tears that, trapped behind my cornea, were unable to raise the alarm by glistening on my cheeks!

9

It was customary in Jacmel to close the casket for the raising and transportation of the body to the church. Just as Scylla Syllabaire was about to shut the lid, my father signalled for him to stop. Paternal clairvoyance allowed me a two-hour reprieve. Everyone seemed to appreciate his infringement of this customary funeral tradition. The good sisters from my school insisted on standing guard over my catafalque, just before the farewells of my closest friends: Sister Nathalie-des-*Anges*, romantic and sensual, her eyes puffy with sorrow in the middle of her impishly charming face; Sister Hortense, the Mother Superior, who seemed a bit ashamed of her tears; Mélissa and Raissa Kraft, the Philisbourg twins, Alina Oriol, Olga Ximilien, Gerda Radsen, and Odile Villèle—all seemed broken like waves on a windless day. Patrick could not stop circling my catafalque, as if my "death" were henceforth to be his cage for life. I had no news of Hector. He must have spent a terrible night in his hospital bed. Once the convoy had departed, a little truck was summoned to load up all the wreaths and bouquets of flowers. I recognized the vehicle as the same one the merchant Sébastien Nassaut used to go around town with, showing off all the gifts that could be purchased at his shop. As we tossed this way and that, my gaze fell on what had been written on the ribbons of the funeral wreaths: *For our darling daughter from the deepest part of our broken hearts,*

Denise and André; For my beloved wife, yours forever, Hector; For the Siloés' Creole fairy, from Prefect Kraft—on behalf of eight thousand heartbroken Jacmelians; From the Sisters of Saint Rose of Lima to their enchanting student; From the women of the iron market to the Siloés' siren; From the tobacco factory workers to the daughter of their employer and benefactor; To the rose in the Good Lord's cap, the team from the Southwest Gazette; *From Patrick to his sister in baptismal water,* among hundreds of others. On the Sorels' balcony, the little boy from the night before threw a fresh rose in my direction. He was aiming for the middle of my chest. I was buried with this talisman. The balconies on Church Street were deserted. The family names came back to me as we moved forward: the Colons, the Maglios, the Bellandes, the Bretouxes, the Claudes, the Craans, the Mételluses, the Wolfs, the Depestres, the Hurbons, the Leroys, the Camilles—whole families moving together toward my burial. Upon arriving at the church, I was happy to see the festive wedding decorations. Deep inside myself, I sang the familiar funeral hymns right along with the Rose of Lima choir.

"Hadriana was her given name," began Father Naélo's sermon.

There was no Sabbath at my wake, Father, aside from the celebration of the Vodou gods paying homage to the beauty of life. God, in His mercy, will not hold a grudge against the *guédés.* Thank You, Father, for spilling the water of Christ on my bare feet, wounded during my very difficult uphill climb. Thank You for "the star that shone only once." Where? When? The night at the holiday resort in Meyer beneath Patrick's awkward, trembling hand? In the garden of the manor, in the respectful arms of my Hector? It feels so sweet to me, praying to the blessed Mary, Mother of God—help all those who have loved me as well as those who have hated me; love my parents in my place, protect my husband Hector, my friends, Mam Diani, and my beloved brother; pray for us poor sinners, now at the hour of death, so be it!

Father Naélo then said tenderly: "Farewell, madame!"

"Farewell, and thank you, Father," I said without anyone hearing me.

10

LEAVING THE CHURCH, I was submerged in intoxicating light. I suddenly felt more weightless than a feather. I had become a wisp of straw in a torrent of rain. On either side of my coffin, strong arms held me securely above the streams of light that marked the final stages of my destiny. The convoy sailed smoothly along without lurching or rolling. Upon reaching Turnier's Shop, Patrick took his uncle's spot at my port side. He only stopped caressing me with his eyes when he in turn was relieved by someone else. I was the eye of a storm blowing in the sunshine. My friends' houses filed by with their familiar physiognomy: I was forever leaving behind the Lapierres, the Lamarques, the Gousses, the Lemoines, the Beaulieus, the Cadets, the Dougés. On the façade of Pinchinat High School, I was greeted by a banner that read: *The Class of 1938 Thanks Nana Siloé for Having Opened Its Imagination to the Beauty of the World.* At the steepest part of the coastline, four masked men abruptly took hold of the coffin, singing and dancing. Instead of progressing forward, they started heading back the way we had come. They moved forward, then in reverse, without deciding one way or the other, as if some invisible danger was holding them back. The convoy started moving backward, then forward, in a single breath, only to move back again with the same momentum, while at the same time the crossbearer and the nuns leading the coffin started getting far ahead of the rest of the burial party. I was the hub of this strange ballet of U-turns and lightning-quick about-faces. What were those guédés up to? Whose path were they trying to confuse? That has remained one of the mysteries of my Jacmelian adventure. The merry-go-round ride finally came to an end in the central path of the cemetery. My father, Prefect Kraft, and Uncle Féfé took back their sad possession from the hands of the death spirits. Then there was a sort of general scattering of the procession. It could have been mistaken for the beginning of a big country festival, a lively picnic where everyone was jockeying for the best spot under the trees on a typical lovely January Sunday. The epitaphs on the gravestones quickly reminded me of the situation I was in: *Here lies Rosena Adonis, taken from her loved ones at the age of thirty-two, RIP; For our marvellous father Sextus Berrouet, division chief, dead in his seventy-ninth year; Here lies Jacmelian Major Seymour Lherisson*; and on a brand-new marble stone: *Here lies, in all her splendour, our cherished mother Germaine Villaret-Joyeuse (1890–1937), requiescat in pace.* I closed my eyes in terror, only opening them upon arrival at the grave site. I was placed right on the ground underneath a gleaming almond tree. The gravediggers seemed fascinated by the client of the day. I saw a shadow of doubt glimmering in one of the diggers' eyes. Lost and without any recourse, I was good and frightened as Father Naélo's drops of holy water fell on my face. I was not doing much better as Maître Homaire began playing a melody from an opera that my mother had played a few times on the piano. Everyone cried while listening to it. My diaphragm contracted, I felt tears forming, creating a knot in my chest. But my "outburst" ended there, well before reaching my throat. The same thing happened when all of Jacmel sang its farewell to me. Lolita's soprano, Uncle

Féfé's bass, the accompaniment of the flute, and the immense wailing chorus were all tearing me apart but were not able to free my tears, imprisoned as they were behind my eyes. In the golden pomp of that Sunday, the words of that song brought me back to a fragile wooden bridge as I crossed Meyer Stream, accompanied by Lolita Philisbourg, who, that summer back then, had taught me a new song: "Sorrowful Sunday." Then there was the sound of a horse galloping, of a cock crowing, of a dog barking, of an adolescent laughing, and of tender chirping in the almond tree. My father waved his handkerchief, Mama smiled at me, leaning over my ersatz cradle. Patrick and the hairdresser Syllabaire tenderly closed the lid of my coffin. The sounds of fistfuls of dirt and flowers rang against my face. An empty, formless void took hold of me.

11

How much time had my blackout lasted? An hour? Two? Five? I will never know. Waking up underground, I was still in the same state of pseudo-death, or pseudo-life. My lungs managed to breathe; the air in my chamber seemed to be refreshing itself regularly. There must have been an airway, if not several, in at least one of its walls. I opened my eyes to an empty darkness, a horrifying absence of space and time, an absolutely brutal obscurity. Little by little, the darkness became my own, my property, my second nature—as much as the little trickle of consciousness that continued to gleam in my head. I was integrated into the very fabric of the savagely obscured earth, into the density and darkness of the Jacemelian soil, well aware of the borders between animal, vegetable, and mineral. I had forgotten about my heart ever since its big breakdown the night before at the church. Was that not it now—making its presence known in a rather extraordinary manner? It began with a simple sound in my chest. Then its beating seemed to rise from the depths of the earth, as if the root of the cosmos and my heart were beating as one to nourish the mysterious language of my return to life. The strange rustling, coming from my blood and from the abyss of the soil, was clamouring for something: it was a coarse demand—a fierce and rudimentary SOS—for a ray of hope, a little more oxygen, a sign from some other soul

buried in the depths of this timeless night. There was nothing
to see. I could only listen. I was nothing more than a listener.
I listened to myself fading away in that wooden cage buried
six feet deep in the earth. I listened to myself dying. Whatever
part of me was still alive was trapped in the absolute blindness
of my subterranean hearth. As punishment for some crime
I had not committed, my life had been thrown into a vast
emptiness without any temporal or spatial link to the outside
world. I was lost in the paralysing void known in Haiti as
zombification. I had been temporarily tossed into the dungeon
of a grave before being divided through black magic into a *gros
bon ange* and a *petit bon ange*, left in a doubly vegetative sham
of an existence: on the one side, a pretty cow's head, infinitely
exploitable and, above all, infinitely fuckable; and on the
other side, lifelong resident of an old, oversized champagne
bottle. That future seemed an even more horrific fate to me
than this primitive auditory existence I had been living since
Saturday night, in this state of catalepsy or bogus death. My
supersonic hearing was on the lookout for ultrasounds. What
I had thought, when I woke up, was a secret pulsation from
the earth, beating in unison with my pulse, soon became a
language quite familiar to my ears. It was not the fullness of
the obscurity of the earth communing with my terror, it was a
different cosmic whispering—the throbbing of the nearby sea
reaching my funerary cellar. It was the mysterious call of the
bay of my childhood, an indescribable summons to travel, to
hope, to act. The sea of Jacmel was driving me secretly back
toward the luminous space of everything I was this close to
losing forever. Victory was still possible over the diabolical
forces that had zombified me. I just had to listen carefully to
everything that had constituted my life up until that point.
The kidnappers were not going to take long to come collect the

package that had been left at this station at the end of the line. Nothing was more pressing than for me to gather together any memories still capable of resisting. I had to remain attentive to the flow of wonderful years lived on Orleans Street, between Toussaint Louverture Square and the bay. The family home had to open doors in the walls of my bogus death. As before, I had to live and listen to myself living. I listened to myself growing out of the depths of my terrifying burrow to reach the sun-drenched Sunday up there, high above my nightmare. So nothing was more urgent than for me to project myself toward the heights of the radiant day as it continued on without me, sparkling on the dense blue waters of the bay of Jacmel. Laid out for my final rest, or for zombiehood, listening intently to the infinity of life, I had to open myself up like the three giant coconut trees that protected the southern façade of our manor, veterans of seven hurricanes...

12

I WAS ABLE to collect what force I had left so as to remain intensely attuned to the tide that endlessly ebbed and flowed with the kernels of my will to live. I was able to stand upright within myself despite the dreadful numbness caused by the zombifying poison coursing through my veins, despite the airless atmosphere. I listened to the living memory of the most wonderful years of my former life echoing in the secret swells of the bay. I escaped the rigid walls of the coffin, my cadaverous stiffness, the horror of my zombie death, the horribly oppressive space. I threw myself into the sun filled Jacmelian outdoors. It was just like those days of childhood or late adolescence when I would lie on the mosaic tiles of my balcony, doors wide open onto the bay, on the lookout for even the slightest stirrings of life. For me, the magic would always begin in the garden. My father, an amateur botanist, had wanted to please us by cultivating not only the plant life particular to Haiti and the Dominican Republic, but flora from all over the Caribbean— from Cuba to Trinidad, passing by Jamaica, Martinique, Guadeloupe, and the entirety of the French Antilles. Thus there was a sample of each and every species of flowering plant blossoming outside our house, from the most humble to the most spectacular: from sea grape to leatherwood; from morning glories to cabbage palmettos; from cinnamon bark, with its smell of cassis, to tree ferns; from miracle leaf to wild plantain; not to mention the silk-cotton trees, bay laurels, amaryllis, rosebushes, orchids, bougainvillea and climbing jasmine, hibiscus, and dwarf palms; and not counting the fruit trees—coconut, guava, Spanish lime, soursop, breadfruit, mango, star apple, lemon, orange, avocado, scarlet plum, tamarind; and so many other species that I counted among my companions—gumbo-limbo, water mampoo, ram goat, cactus pear, mimosa, all manner of magnolia, breaknail, and mountain blueberry. All the flora of the Caribbean imaginary was in my sight and within my reach, leaving me susceptible to their intoxicating fragrances from morning till night. With its hundreds of species, our garden was a sort of botanical feast— as representative of the coast as of the mountains, of the wildest forest as of the tamest, most well-manicured garden. At the age of sixteen, I impudently parodied a Surrealist poet, taking his macho modernist lyricism and making it feminine: *If there was anything strange about the young girl, about her wandering and vagabond nature, it easily could have been summed up in the two syllables of the word* garden.

Everything in me—the spirit of childhood, a voracious sensuality, the Haitian gift for wonderment, the impulsive humour of the French, all my joy at being in the world— curved my back (and even more lyrically curved my buttocks) there before the trees and the sun-drenched hedges of our garden. On days when the sun was just too overwhelming, I would hang my drowsiness on the cool vines, and my flesh itself, which felt like it was nearly on fire, would become the refreshing liana that my most fervent daydreams would climb up. The grass was soft beneath my bare feet as it sloped gently down toward the water's edge! The shadows were cool and tender on the mango trees at noon. All my adolescent dreams were perfumed by the smells of that garden. Just as others might head aimlessly down any number of roads, testing their vagabond love of life by visiting diverse climates, all I needed to do to sample all of life's finest and most joyful passions was head down to our garden! I listened to and took stock of the manor house: neither town house nor traditional provincial home, it was a two-story dream house, its facade dotted by large windows with adjustable blinds and by ironwork balconies. Its fortress-like walls enclosed large, airy rooms, cosily charming, reflecting a Creole taste and style—bright during the day, illuminated at night by bronze and glass flower-patterned lamps. Such was the "Siloé Manor." Yet I never had the sense of living in a "seigneurial dwelling—some kind of little country castle." I never felt like the chatelaine of an old manor waiting at her window for some "knight with a white feather galloping on his black steed." But if ever there were, in the 1930s, a place on earth at once real and ideal, that was built for living and dreaming one's life, it was that house—situated at a distance from every other one, just below the central square, between the Bel-Air and Seaside neighbourhoods in Jacmel. From the ground floor to the attic, following the house's enchantment up the stairs and down the corridors, from one room to the next, the rustic jalousies opened onto infinity just as the windows opened onto the garden and the bay. From the sitting room to the terraces, from the bedrooms to the pantry, from the cellar to the dining room, from the laundry room to the bathrooms, from the veranda to the library, a windmill of dreams, a generator of magical electricity, created a current of wonder that sent a flow of mysteries, great and small, to tweak and regulate the changing of my seasons. But above all, the manor's baroque charm—so apparent in its mahogany, *acajou*, and rattan furnishings, as well as in every small decorative object made of ivory, silver, porcelain, or opal—was most fascinating to me in the wing where the kitchen and communal spaces were situated. From my earliest childhood until the age of nineteen, these spaces were the true crossroads of my fantasies and my constant state of giddiness. They attracted me less because of the culinary delights being concocted there or the melancholy sleepiness that inevitably followed the midday and evening meals. It was more the fact that it was always there, in the glow of the charcoal stoves, that Haiti began for me. That was where I would go to find Felicia, my personal maid, Sister Yaya the head cook, old Merisier the gardener, Lil' Boucan the houseboy, and three other servants appointed to take care of the household, do the shopping, make the desserts and sorbets, or to perform whatever other minor tasks came up. Together, the seven of them made up "our surrogate indigenous family" (as Mama used to say), affectionate and obliging. They had given themselves the responsibility of satisfying my daily hunger for a dose of something marvellous that took hold of me like a visceral need, not unlike the desire to drink, pee, or sleep. In their eyes, a blond spirit named General Marvellous lived inside Miss Nana. Whenever he possessed her, be it in the kitchen or in the intimacy of her bedroom, everything else came to an abrupt halt, and she had to be given, as Sister Yaya used to say, "dewdrops to drink and Erzili herbs to eat." Out of the stories told to me day and night, the mythology of Vodou entered into my life. The gods, the dances, the drums—none of it held any mystery for me until the moment when one of its lecherous butterflies, controlled by some secret society, poured zombie poison into some icy lemonade on my wedding day.

13

ALL DURING THAT fateful and disastrous Sunday, my fabulous past cleared a passage from the sea all the way to my shipwrecked consciousness. In that narrow space, dark as a well, where I had been immobilized, the tangled skein of my happy memories unravelled slowly and completely, pressing me to embrace hopefulness and to stay vigilant as I waited for whatever was to come that night. I waited patiently, without any sense of time, buffeted by hazy reminiscences and by the lapping of floating recollections. There was nothing else standing between me and overwhelming despair. Nothing to counter my own sense of what was happening. I must have lost consciousness and reawakened several times. During one of these brief respites, I had the feeling that the pincers of some necrophagous insect were nibbling away at the wall of silence that enveloped me. Then it felt as if the dirt covering my coffin was getting lighter. I was not mistaken: before long, a metal shovel was striking at the roof of my cage; soon afterward, the lid shifted. Strong arms lifted me by the shoulders and feet. That first brutal contact with the fresh air was almost suffocating. I was able to make out the silhouette of three men around my open grave. In addition to the two who had disinterred me, a third man stood in the background, his eyes fixed on me. He seemed a great deal older than the others. He was a thick-necked Haitian man, broad-shouldered and massive. He wore a machete in his belt and held a long whip in his hand. He shouted my name three times, in a thunderous voice, as if he had to use all of his strength to call for me.

"Hadriana Siloé, goddamnit!" he yelled the third time.

He took a few steps toward me. He crouched down at my side. He looked at me for a moment before slapping me hard enough to draw blood. Seeming satisfied, he sat down on a grave and hoisted my upper body onto his lap. He then brought a flask to my lips. A thick, heavily lemon-scented liquid ran over my clenched teeth. After a brief pause, he had me drink more of the antidote. As I swallowed, an intense heat coursed through me—first my lower limbs, then my entire body began to awaken, infused with newly oxygenated blood. I could move my tongue once I had imbibed the last sips of the zombiemaker's drug.

"Feeling better, my little pussycat?" he said.

I was able to nod my head. For a brief moment I forgot that I was in the arms of one of Baron-Samedi's henchmen. The smell of maleness, of fresh earth, and of the impending storm all helped to restore my vitality like a blessing.

"With a nice piece of woman like yourself, things will move along quick and easy," he said. "This is a homemade potion that Papa Rosanfer is using for the first time, made specially for his *petit bon ange* from France!"

With that, he leaned over me and grabbed the hem of my wedding dress. He parted my knees, all the while talking into my ear with his raspy, searing voice.

"From now on, everything that's right-side up in your white woman's existence will be turned upside down and made black, starting with your name: *Hadriana Siloé* is no good for a zombie; there's too much white salt in that name. My turn to baptise you: *Eolis Anahir-dah!* Now that is a fitting name for Papa Rosanfer's dark *femme-jardin*. Yes, I, Don Rosalvo Rosanfer—great man of Haut-Cap-Rouge before the eternal Baron-Samedi—I am now the master of your back door! Eolis, Lil' Lilisse, Sweet Lil'Dah, ohoho! It's already nice and sunny under there. It's already well past noon under these veils. I'm turning everything in your life upside down, except, except... except what—can you guess? Cat got your tongue? Of course, you have no idea..."

All this time, his fingers were moving crablike and feverishly up my thighs.

"Except for this!" he said, brutally flattening his peasant's hand against my ripe almond. "Talk about a flowering plant in the hands of a magic gardener! Hello there, flower-of-the-rising-sun! Greetings, sweet peach of Queen Erzili-Fréda! Congratulations, Madame Rosalvo! My friends, ohoho! This bride has a set of twin gods under her veils! A veritable zombie-mattress for General Rosanfer! Twin fruits, filled out in two places—why, hello there!"

After this outburst, he pulled himself together. He gave me a friendly tap on the bottom and gently propped me up against a tomb. He then turned to his companions, who had been standing off to the side.

"Let's hurry this up! Looks like rain's coming. Bring the horses quickly."

His accomplices gone, the man looked up at the rapidly darkening sky and then exclaimed: "This is going to be much worse than a little sun-shower! We're looking at a big-mamaood of a storm. We're going to have to rush those beasts along. You're a good rider, right?"

At that exact moment, I looked at myself in my inside mirror and said: *Let's go, Hadriana!* Without waiting a second longer, I leaped up in a flash and took to my heels, my athlete's blood and endangered life right there alongside me. Losing Papa Rosafer among the graves was child's play. I had not gone a hundred yards before it began to rain: not a little sprinkle, but one of those torrential storms I had loved as a young girl. Seeking shelter in a small mausoleum, I took a few moments to remove everything that could hinder my getaway: my high heels, bridal veil, and train. I tied the whole package around my waist and plunged headlong out into the downpour. I knew that graveyard like the back of my hand. To get out of there, I avoided the main path and gate. I took a shortcut that led to the friars' school in Petite Batterie. Once I made it there, I quickly crossed the street and picked up my pace, taking another detour. Just as I had done so many times before, I inched closer and closer to Bel-Air. I did not even feel the deadly exhaustion of the past day and night. A sort of animal strength propelled me forward through the deluge that, although it blurred my vision, could not distract me from the single-minded intention that was spurring me on: escape from zombification. Should I head straight to my family home? Instinctively, I thought that would be a huge mistake. My pursuers would be waiting to ambush me there, or patrolling the deserted edges of the property and the town square. An idea came to me a few yards from the prison: why not seek refuge in there? What safer harbour was there for a young girl being chased in the middle of the night by a trio of criminal sorcerers?

"Halt! Who goes there?" shouted the guard on duty as I approached.

He recognized me as soon as he saw me standing there in the rain. He let out a scream of astonishment and dropped his rifle. Teeth chattering, he closed the gate from the inside before running away with the keys.

Then it was my turn to scream: "Help! I'm being chased by a bunch of murderers! Open up!"

Not a soul appeared. I went back up the long hill to the market. Threading my way through the stands and metal vaults, I headed toward the same church I had left feet first fifteen hours earlier. I took a passageway that opened onto the main entrance of the rectory. The gate was closed. The driving rain drowned out my cries. I picked up some pebbles and threw them vainly at Father Naélo's balcony and shutters. Water blocked my nose, mouth, and ears—it was as if I myself was one with the thunder and rain. Taking the same narrow path that bordered the church, I retraced my steps back toward the iron market. I took shelter under its roof and tried to catch my breath. I remembered my friends the Altamonts: Patrick lived with Mam Diani's brother, Uncle Féfé. If I took Church Street, I could get to Bourbon Street in just a couple of minutes. Furious gusts of wind deepened the shadows all around me. I moved forward from balcony to balcony, avoiding the central alleyway. Overcome with joy, I made my way up the path to the steps of the magistrate's house. I literally threw myself on the door and pounded with both fists. I waited for several minutes, knocking for what seemed like forever... in vain.

14

I KNOCKED ON the doors of nearly all the houses on the northern edge of the square, including the iron doors of the prefecture where my friends the Krafts resided, and on the doors of the Star Café—all in vain. Across the way, at the convent, I threw fistfuls of gravel at the windows, to no avail. I could have climbed the walls of the school and hidden safely in that familiar place until daybreak. But instead I decided to risk crossing the square and navigating the two hundred or so yards separating me from my family home. I stopped for a moment at the music pavilion and peered into the surrounding darkness before plunging through the diagonal sheets of rain. I arrived at the doorway of the manor house within moments. Out of breath, I desperately rang the bell. A great surge of hope passed through me: I heard steps and voices in the corridor on the ground floor. I waited for several minutes with my finger glued to the doorbell. Suddenly, a flash of lightning cleared away the darkness: in that second, I was able to make out three men on horseback at the end of Orleans Street, coming toward me at full tilt. Gasping with fear, I dashed off in the opposite direction toward a narrow passage where a set of natural stairs tumbled down the length of the fence bordering our property. I took them four at a time, at breakneck speed, and finally reached Main Street. I shot across the road, planning to plead for protection from the sentinels at the police headquarters. I found myself face to face with the two sentries standing watch there. On seeing me, one of them passed out immediately—right in the sentry box. The other one pulled the trigger of his Springfield. Too scared to aim properly, he missed me. In the time it had taken me to get from the prison to the barracks, the rain had put the finishing touches on my horrifying appearance. I picked up my pace and avoided Saint Anne's Street, cutting across a corridor that led to the beach. The sea, whipped into a violent frenzy by the storm, was a dark, raging cauldron. Its savage rumblings drowned out the sound of the rain. I wanted nothing more than to bite into its nocturnal fury—a fury as strong as the will to live that nourished each one of my freely taken steps as a woman "brought back" from the dead. I headed into the breaking waves: with overwhelming zeal I breathed in the aroma of salt and gulped down a mouthful of water that was even cooler than the rain still pouring over me. I walked along the shore, heading west. The wet sand was pure heaven compared to the hard surface of the streets. I forged ahead in a whirl of confusion and despair. It was unbelievable: in less than twenty-four hours, my name no longer opened any doors in Jacmel, not even that of my own home. I had been shot at without warning. That was all I could think of until finally reaching the first steep slopes of La Voûte Mountain. Not at all out of breath, I climbed the same paths I used to crisscross on horseback, either alone or with my parents. The regions of Haut Gandou, Trou Mahot, and Fond Melon were perfectly familiar to me. The storm faded amidst the clearings that had opened up in the predawn skies. Vegetation was spread out across the landscape, having freed itself from the scores of moist shadows as daylight fell over the groves of banana, coffee, and orange trees. On several occasions, flocks of guinea fowl, wood pigeons, and ortolan buntings flew out of the rain-soaked bushes growing on the sides of the road, their wings still drenched with rain. I managed to keep up the brisk pace of those adolescent hikes until the sun rose. I walked with a long, supple gait—that easy way of undulating and swaying that I had learned as a child from the dark-skinned canephors that lined the valley in Jacmel. I had resolved to reach the village of Bainet and to call my parents from there. They would take the paved road to come get me. I had already dealt with what was most important: I had ditched my kidnappers. From the very first moments after regaining my freedom, I felt that my ordeal had anchored me even more squarely in my existence. From then on I would know, a thousand times better than before, how to fill every hour of each day and each night in the future, which was my greatest dream after the experience of death. To have had my horizon so frighteningly suspended between death and life would make my existence at once more dynamic and more sensitive to the delicately complex doings of my fellow man. My connections to the sea, the sky, the birds, the rain, the trees, and the wind had been forever fortified, just as my most vital senses had become better attuned to both animals and human beings. I would do a far better job of listening to all aspects of my feminine voice, though always well aware, from that morning on, that while the natural woman may have been reborn from these trials more capable of fully savouring every moment, the woman I was in society would never completely recover from the wounds on her hands made by all the doors she had knocked on that night. The main thing was having escaped safe and sound from my zombification. Those hours of rigorous effort had done my body a lot of good. I felt as if I had flushed out most of the zombie poison as well as the antidote that had gotten me back on my feet. Something had gone wrong in Papa Rosanfer's calculations. He had not managed to capture my *petit bon ange*. Is it possible he confused it with the *gros bon ange* of my sex? The idea made me laugh. What an extraordinary delight it was simply to be able to laugh in the boundless, sun-drenched morning air. My burst of laughter was so clear that it seemed to have been filtered underground through the crystal of a mountain spring. Its streaming waters refreshed my degraded and injured flesh. Emerging from a banana grove, I found myself in the Haut-Coq-qui-Chant section of Jacmel. There was the sea, spread out before me in the morning light: dense and flat, superbly clear blue, and already calm after the violence of the night before. At the same time I discovered, near the steep and twisted shoreline, the cheerful plains of Bainet, stretched around the crescent of a sparkling bay. What must I have looked like in my tattered wedding dress, with its flounces flattened and its train and veil rolled up around my hips like a defeated life preserver? Spattered with stains and stuck to my skin, the layers of tulle and lace looked like a dirty, pitiful, and ragged old piece of gauze. I wanted to fix up my zombie getup as much as possible before I ran into any living souls in broad daylight. More or less tidying up my outfit, I found myself surprised in a way that fit perfectly with the outrageous surrealism of my adventure. An envelope containing my dowry was in the little purse attached to my belt. It contained several thousand-dollar bills, and a prophetic note written on my father's calling card: *For our Nana on her wedding day, we offer this modest sum for a rainy day.* My second surprise turned out to be the welcome I received from the inhabitants of Bainet. On the tip of a peninsula just outside of the coastal village, I was carefully making my way down a rocky path that led to a small cove, when I noticed a group of men and women heatedly conversing around a large sailboat anchored between two rocks. When they heard the noise of my timid footsteps, they stopped talking and followed my progress, their expressions friendly and attentive. They were far from shocked by my strange appearance. In fact, the closer I got to them, the more their faces shone with marvel, as if my outfit, shabby testament to the shipwreck of my wedding day, was for them the revelation of a fascinating mystery.

"Hello, everyone," I said.

"Hello, Your Majesty," they responded in chorus. "Might you have a bit of water to spare, my friends? I'm terribly thirsty."

My words were received with peals of laughter. "Just some water?" asked one of the peasant women. "Isn't all of this yours?"

With her arm, she traced a wide circle that encompassed the inlet, the sailboat, the coconut grove, the sea, and even the sun that shone on that January day.

A young woman held out a calabash to me. As soon as I took hold of it, a stocky and mischievous black man pushed it aside. "Coconut water is more fitting for Her Majesty Simbi-la-Source!"

He rushed over to one of the coconut trees on the shore, quickly climbed to the top, and brought down a cluster of coconuts. With a blow from his machete, he split one open and gave it to me after executing a low bow. My head thrown back, facing the sunny cove, I let the clear, fragrant, bittersweet water flood into me in intoxicating waves. After I had emptied the coconut in a single gulp, the man immediately offered me another, while his friends improvised a song in my honour:

Simbi-la-Source, wa-yo!

Simbi has emerged from the unknown
to bless our great sailboat.
Simbi is the head and the belly
of the third bank of the waters!
What a beautiful morsel of a woman
Is that Simbi-la-Rosée, wa-yo!

My death was cleared out of my veins entirely. The generosity of these people flooded me with a lust for life. Each new gulp brought back to my body and soul a sense of the woman who was being born for a second time within me. After drinking several coconuts in a row, literally blinded by the flowing water, I said, "I don't know how to thank you," placing a hand on my purse.

"No, you don't owe us anything. Where are you headed?" asked an old man.

"What about you all?" I replied.

"A few of us are emigrating to Jamaica. The journey only takes a day and a half at most. Would you like to accompany them, Your Majesty?"

"Happily! Yes, yes, yes, I'll leave with them forever," I said, tracing a few dance steps in the sand to the applause of my hosts.

These are the circumstances in which I arrived in Port Antonio, at dawn on February 3, 1938, having made the decision to cut all ties with my Jacmelian past. It was the first time that Immigration Services in Jamaica had ever seen a young white woman disembark with a bunch of Haitians, veritable pariahs of the Caribbean wherever they migrated in search of work. Profoundly flustered by my presence, the British agents pretended to believe the story my travel companions had already been spreading: I was Simbi-la-Source. The gods of

Vodou had charged me with the task of escorting a handful of Jacmelian emigrants to Jamaica. Goddess or whore, I wouldn't have had any trouble obtaining a lifetime resident's permit in any island of the archipelago. In those days, white skin and blond hair, better than any diplomatic passport, were worth as much as a visa of divine right. But that is a whole other story. In these notes, I only hope to describe fifteen hours of the false death of a woman desperately, passionately, fatally in love with life.

15

FOR THE RECORD

Having told our two tales, Hadriana and I could have added, as an epilogue to the memoirs brought together here, the story of the ten years we have since spent as a happy couple. Yet, although not entirely convinced, we have decided to take it on faith that the travails and splendours of love have, in fact, no story...

THE END

GLOSSARY OF TERMS

Agoué-Taroyo: Vodou god, master of the sea and its islands.

Ange: French word for angel. In this novel, it refers to the notion that each individual contains two forces—two souls—within him or her: the *petit bon ange* and the *gros bon ange*.

Apo lisa gbadia tâmerra dabô!: Magic spell in African dialect.

Baka: Evil spirit in the service of sorcerers.

Banda: Fast-paced dance that mimics, at once, the acts of death and copulation.

Baron-Samedi: Principle god of death, father of the guédés.

Bizango: Member of a secret society dealing in black magic.

Cadavre-collectif: Moment in the *rada* dance, after a casser-tambour, in which the crowd freezes in imitation of a cadaver.

Caraco: Long, beltless, one-piece tunic once worn by elderly women in Haiti.

Charles-Oscar: Former Minister of the Interior, known for his cruelty, who is represented as a devil during carnival.

Dahomey: Former kingdom in western Africa; now southern Benin.

Damballah-Ouèdo: God of springs and rivers, he holds a high position among the loas of the *rada* ritual.

Erzili (or Erzili-Fréda): Goddess of love and beauty, guardian of freshwater; she is invoked under the name of Fréda Toucan-Dahomin, sometimes linked to the Mater Dolorosa.

Femme-jardin: Literally translates to "garden woman"; can mean mistress; can mean one of a man's several wives who may live separately from him; or can mean a man's favored or most beloved female companion.

Guédé: Spirit of death who plays a major role in sorcery.

HASCO: Haitian American Sugar Company, a North American sugar company established in Haiti.

Homo Papadocus: Papa Doc (François Duvalier, Haitian tyrant from 1957 to 1971), well known for his Tonton-Macoutes, the regime's "bogeyman" militia.

Houngan: Vodou priest

Jacques the Major (saint): Linked in Vodou to the loa Ogou, patron of blacksmiths, god of armies.

Loa: Supernatural being in Vodou; more than a god or divinity, a *loa* can be a bene cial or a harmful spirit.

Maître: Literally translates to master in English. In French, the term Maître is used in front of one's name like Mister, but designates that the person is a male lawyer.

Makandal, François: Famous eighteenth-century Maroon leader; a makandal is also a talisman.

Mambo: Vodou priestess.

Maroons: African slaves of West Indies and Guiana in the seventeenth and eighteenth centuries, who escaped from slavery and established their own communities.

Nago-grand-coup: Rhythm of a warrior dance marked by undulating movements, hands on the knees, face thrusting forward and back as if to break the torso against some sort of obstacle.

Ouidah: Beach in Benin, formerly Dahomey, where human cargo—"ebony wood"—was loaded onto ships during the time of the Atlantic slave trade.

Rabordaille: Fast-paced carnival dance set to the beating of a small cylindrical drum with two layers of skin.

Rada: Refers to a family of gods and to the rituals associated with them (word originates from the village of Allada in Benin).

Sectes aux yeux rouges: Translates into English as red-eyed sects; it refers to the various factions who follow the practices of witchcraft, including: *zobop, bizango, Vlanbindingue,* and others.

Simbi (or Simbi-la-Source): A white *loa,* goddess of the rains and beauty.

Tête-gridape: Individual with kinky hair; by extension, the word applies to a small lamp with a smoky wick.

Tonton-Macoutes: The Duvalier regime's "bogeyman" militia—a sort of tropical SS.

Vaksin: A bamboo trumpet-like instrument popular in Haiti.

Vlanbindingues: Brotherhood of sorcerers whose members are supposedly bound together by acts of sorcery committed as a group.

Vodou: Popular Haitian religion born of the syncretism of rites originating in sub-Saharan Africa and Catholic beliefs; it is an agrarian cult that plays the same role in Haitian life as that of pagan sects in ancient societies.

Vertières: On November 18, 1803, in Vertières in northern Haiti, General Donatien de Rochambeau, leader of the expeditionary French forces, surrendered to Haitian General Jean-Jacques Dessalines's revolutionary army. This was the first battle the French lost in the history of colonization.

Yanvalou-dos-bas: A lively, cheerful dance performed with a hunched back and one's hands on bent knees while rolling one's shoulders in an undulating motion.

Zozo: Vulgar Creole slang for penis.

TRANSLATOR'S NOTE

Hadriana in All My Dreams is a classic of Haitian letters. First published in 1988, the novel won the French Prix Renaudot, along with several other prestigious prizes. Almost immediately following its publication in French, it was translated into Danish, German, Spanish, Italian, Dutch, and Polish. Surprisingly, though, Hadriana has never been published in its entirety in English until now. This, I suspect, may have something to do with the novel's shameless eroticism. Yes, there is more sex than politics in this narrative, at least on the surface, and perhaps certain clichés about Anglophone Puritanism hold true (guring out how to translate Depestre's twenty or so terms for human genitalia indeed had me stretching the limits of the English language). But if Depestre's narrative foregrounds the sexual and the sensual within the frame of the marvellous, it is also a sophisticated work of social satire. *Hadriana* evokes the complexities of race, gender, and religion with which Haitians have long grappled; it reflects the author's fraught relationship with a home he inhabits solely through the detritus of memory and the gift of his imagination.

Bringing this novel to English-speaking audiences has particular resonance for me, a Caribbean literature scholar teaching in a New York City institution. New York is one of the primary sites of the Haitian diaspora and, as such, many of my students are first-generation Haitian Americans who read and write in English—not French. And so I've been a firsthand witness to the broader phenomenon whereby a transnational population is cut off from certain aspects of its cultural heritage. Insofar as René Depestre is an incontrovertible pillar of the Haitian literary canon, his extraordinary contribution to world letters ought to be read by all who can claim him as one of their own.

—Kaiama L. Glover

ABOUT THE AUTHOR

René Depestre, born in 1926, is one of the most important voices of Haitian literature. A peer of seminal figures Aimé Césaire, Pablo Neruda, and André Breton, Depestre has engaged with the politics/aesthetics of negritude, social realism, and surrealism for more than half a century. Having lived through significant moments in Haitian and New World history—from the overthrow of Haitian dictator Élie Lescot in 1946, to the first Congress of Black Writers and Artists in Paris in 1956, to a struggle with Haiti's François "Papa Doc" Duvalier in 1957, to a collaboration with Cuban revolutionary Che Guevara and a fraught relationship with Fidel Castro in the 1960s and '70s—Depestre is uniquely positioned to reflect on the extent to which the Americas and Europe are implicated in Haiti's past and present.

ABOUT THE TRANSLATOR

Kaiama L. Glover is an associate professor of French and Africana Studies at Barnard College, Columbia University. She is the author of *Haiti Unbound: A Spiralist Challenge to the Postcolonial Canon*, coeditor of *Yale French Studies' Revisiting Marie Vieux-Chauvet: Paradoxes of Postcolonial Feminine* (issue no. 128), and translator of Frankétienne's *Ready to Burst* and Marie Vieux-Chauvet's *Dance on the Volcano*. She has received awards from the National Endowment for the Humanities, the Mellon Foundation, and the Fulbright Foundation.